THE MACKENZIE EXPERIMENTS

<u>BOOK ONE</u>
RUMOR OF THE YEAR

DILLON FLAKE

Dedicated to my wonderful and supportive wife, Emily

CHAPTER ONE
THE MACKENZIE EXPERIMENTS

There are no books about Mackenzie, Idaho. It is home to 800 people, a dozen small businesses, and a length of river bent in the shape of a horseshoe. Even on the most detailed maps of Idaho, it appears as no more than a tiny black dot with an 8-point-font label. Most Idahoans have never heard of Mackenzie, and those who have know it only as a place they've driven through. There are never relatives, friends, or even acquaintances to stop and see. It's just a little nothing town you pass in and out of on your way to McCall or Donnelley or places like that.

Still, growing up there I always thought it had just enough rustic charm to be the subject of someone's pastoral. It's got all the dirt and denim and unrefined colloquial of a Western with none of the excitement. It's a good place to live if you've always wanted to own too many dogs and have a yard full of trucks that don't work.

I always felt its appeal was in its predictability. As long as you never expected surprises you were never disappointed. We always anticipated green grass from May to June and snow from Halloween to Easter. The state took care of plowing the main road running through town because it was a highway—a long, meandering highway that was barren for most of the year until camping season. Counting the highway, Mackenzie had only one paved road to speak of. And one traffic light, a flashing yellow one. It was the only traffic light in Boise County.

It should come as no surprise that one-traffic-light towns like Mackenzie thrive on rumors. Prosaic daily life welcomes embellishment. In a place twenty miles from the nearest movie theater, shopping mall, or chain restaurant, hearsay ranks as one of the most popular forms of entertainment—competing only with hunting and jumping in the river. There is an atmosphere in such towns that affords rumors unnaturally long life. Many feel, even unconsciously, a pressure to nurture an exciting, bizarre, or scandalous story in defiance of a humdrum reality. Sometimes rumors are the *only* things that change in Mackenzie.

In short, of its own accord Mackenzie was not a place of great significance. It is ironic that, after such an undistinguished career, it would serve as the setting for a true story unparalleled by any rumor in its past. Nobody knew then that this obscure Idaho town would be home to some of the strangest and most remarkable events in human history—events that would challenge mankind's sense of superiority.

I played only a limited role, yet there are few people born to Earthly parents who can claim the authority that I can regarding the Mackenzie Experiments, interstellar telepathy, or a small planet across the universe called Kalaxzos.

I admit I know most of what I do about the Mackenzie Experiments only secondhand. Others have produced partial histories, most notably Aurora Noel and Dr. Hiram Yafa. I have had the opportunity to read both obscure works only through my association with both Aurora and Dr. Yafa. Aurora's took the form of a manifesto that was submitted to the Idaho Statesman shortly before her disappearance but was never published, and Yafa's was so exhaustive that it remained unfinished at the time of his death.

A third source provided the bulk of the information used for this volume. It was a controversial article entitled *I Was Antonia LeBlanc*, written by an Oregon native named Phoebe Rhodes. Like Aurora, Rhodes had submitted her narrative to various news outlets during the related international tumult that preceded my own abduction. It was largely ignored by the media initially, firstly because it was far too long to print and secondly because its claims were so outrageous that they were sure to be false. But when the titular Antonia LeBlanc was asked about the sparsely-published article in a TV interview she would not deny its authenticity. An abridged version of Rhodes' narrative soon appeared in every news outlet in the country, the first public confession of a fantastic secret that was then nearly twenty years old.

Knowing what I do now about the long history of the Mackenzie Experiments I suppose I could start anywhere. I'm starting as Phoebe did: with the incidents that revolved largely around Atlas Ranch. The reason for choosing this point as my Genesis will become clearer as more of this bizarre timeline is revealed. Otherwise, as unusual as this episode was, the secrecy surrounding it has made it almost as obscure as the decades of experimentation preceding it. It was simply another part in the elaborate 1,000-piece puzzle that makes up the secret history of Mackenzie, Idaho.

This is a fitting metaphor, as 1,000-piece puzzles were a favorite hobby of Jim Boyd, the Mackenzie resident who owned and operated the ranch. Jim had a number of puzzles framed and hung on the walls at Atlas Ranch. There were seventeen of them, each Western or farm themed except for one of a world map, which hung over the fireplace. He'd completed each of them single-handedly and was about a third of the way through another. Juan and Axl were helping him with this one. Axl was only fourteen and found puzzles tedious and unfulfilling but he loved his Uncle Jim and never brought it up.

Axl's summertime visits had been a tradition since he was ten. Axl's father—Jim's younger brother—drove him to Idaho to spend a month or two working at Atlas Ranch and keeping Jim company. Axl felt sorry for his uncle: he'd been living alone for a long time. In-between Axl's infrequent contact with Uncle Jim throughout the year, he entertained the grim vision of his beloved uncle deteriorating into a reclusive and senile Ben Gunn. Yet, whenever they were reunited, Uncle Jim was always the same thin, gray, Wrangler-wearing rancher, unchanged from year to year. He and his little Idaho town seemed frozen in time.

The only thing that ever *did* change was the ranch. Jim had been ranching for even longer than he'd been alone, and every few years he'd get antsy. Sometime in the elapsed year Uncle Jim had decided to turn the ranch into a country retreat. He planned to rent it out for anniversaries, business getaways, and family reunions. "Just perfect for an old guy like me that doesn't want to do *real* work anymore," he kept saying. Jim hoped to have all his planned renovations completed by fall. Axl learned a lot about wood and nails that summer.

He also learned a little bit of Spanish from Juan, a gifted builder that Jim had hired on for the project. Juan had a talkative and buoyant way that made long hot days of summer labor pass by almost too quickly. Axl knew he would always remember that summer, if only as a disorderly collection of sensations and images: icy sodas in glass bottles, crickets that sounded like rattlesnakes, pickup trucks with the windows rolled down, and dirt so embedded in his hands that no amount of washing could get rid of it.

CHAPTER TWO
THE RANCHER

It was the evening of the Fourth of July that summer and Axl and Uncle Jim had long since stopped working for the day. It was a singular scene in the mind of a fourteen-year-old boy: spending Independence Day in the country, on the roof of a ranch house, waiting for the fireworks to start. Uncle Jim was nothing less than a cowboy in Axl's eyes, and probably a frontier hero in his younger years. It came as no great surprise when his uncle suggested watching the fireworks from the roof and brought up all the snacks in the cupboard and all the sodas left in the fridge. If Jim had kicked the ladder down and declared the rooftop their new home, Axl wouldn't have minded in the least.

Jim was sharing a strip of homemade jerky with Brodie, his border collie. Axl considered his luck in having Jim for an uncle. He had some difficulty believing that Jim and his father were brothers. Axl's life was, it seemed to him, a very prosaic one indistinct from that of any other teenager living in the suburbs of Seattle. His father seemed intentionally to choose cars, houses, clothes, and careers that kept life from becoming too interesting. Of course Axl loved his father, but there seemed to be no semblance between the homebody banker and the squinty-eyed cowboy sitting with Axl on the roof. Jim was right out of a Western: a lean, built man with a denim jacket, a gray-brown mustache, and skin turned to leather by the sun. He even had a drawl that he'd picked up from years of association with Texas cattlemen. He lacked only the colorful dialogue, which Axl suspected Jim kept hidden until after he had gone home to Washington. Jim was careful always about cursing around women and kids. Still, Axl had once or twice tried to draw it out of his Uncle by swearing himself, only to be reprimanded.

Uncle Jim had the air of a man who had had some adventures, even if those days were over. Axl often fantasized that he'd be just like Uncle Jim when he was sixty—rugged, tan, fit, confident, well-liked, and independent. The only difference would be living somewhere other than Mackenzie. Mackenzie seemed an unfitting place for a Western hero to retire. Axl had already decided that, someday when he wrote his memoirs, the chapter about Mackenzie would be called *The Nothingest Town in the World.* It felt slow and lifeless to Axl—a place with the prevailing air of a truck stop. Outside the cowboy wonderland that Atlas Ranch was, Mackenzie seemed to be a rogue's gallery of rednecks and hicks. They were friendly enough, most of them. Occasionally Uncle Jim would interact with someone coarse and unpleasant enough to meet with his disapproval. But true to his good nature, the only criticism Jim would ever offer was, "That guy sure is a talker!"

Jim talked too, of course, but seemed uncommonly comfortable with silence. He wasn't excitable or high-strung at all. Axl had once knocked an entire bowl of potato salad out of the kitchen window into the yard, breaking the bowl and ruining the salad. Axl had felt terrible, but Uncle Jim had taken one look at the accident and said, "Leave it. The ants have been looking kind of slim lately."

Jim was also very smart, Axl found out, and never seemed to forget anything. The minutia he retained was superhuman: license plate numbers, birthdays, statistics, song lyrics. One time Axl's MP3 player had shuffled to LFO's *Summer Girls* while they were driving somewhere and Uncle Jim had sung along with the entire song. "How many times have you heard this song?" Axl had asked.

"Once, back in the 90's," Uncle Jim replied, "it was playing at the gas station." Jim might have been just as surprised that Axl knew the song, but Axl often spoke of his love for "old school stuff."

The only memory Jim couldn't seem to place was that of a strange ornament on his keychain. Jim thought it was a piece of jewelry, but it might also have been a coin—it was only barely larger than a quarter. It was triangular in shape, with one point barely exceeding the other two in length. It seemed to be made of white gold but had a vague bluish tint and had three perfectly-circular holes stamped in a row down the middle. Jim couldn't remember where it came from but he thought it had belonged to his late wife Jessica, so he'd laced a little chain through the large middle hole and linked it to his keys.

Jim was wrong about the coin, though: it hadn't been given to Jessica, it had been given to him. But the giver hadn't intended for him to remember.

All that July day Uncle Jim had been celebrating the nation's independence by recounting trivia about the revolution, the lives of presidents, and even the science behind aerials. As Axl sat on the roof that night, crunching up fistfuls of cashews and sunflower seeds and beef jerky in defiance of his braces, Uncle Jim was explaining something about horses.

Axl's face spread with a satisfied grin as he relished the moment. He wasn't really listening—Uncle Jim talked about horses a lot, and Axl was prone to a wandering mind. He was ranking this day against other "Best Days Ever" he'd had at the ranch. The incessant hum of a million invisible insects seemed an ode to his boyish euphoria. Overhead the sky was slowly fading, its weary blue glow dimming to reveal a pantheon of distant planets and stars. Axl couldn't remember a night when there seemed to be so many, like a celestial connect-the-dots that would take centuries to complete. Uncle Jim noted his fascination.

"You know they shine brighter here than anywhere else, right?" the old rancher mused.

"I was just thinking that," Axl replied. "Why is that? Is the elevation a lot higher here than it is back home?"

"Probably," Jim said. "But I think it's got more to do with light pollution than it does with elevation. I don't know that a few thousand feet would make much of a difference. Proxima Centauri is the closest star to the Earth other than the Sun and it's more than four light-years away."

"How far is that?"

"Well, the fastest spaceship we've ever launched does better than 24,000 miles an hour. If NASA let us borrow it we'd leave tomorrow and get to Proxima in about 100,000 years."

"Whoa!" Axl exclaimed.

"…give or take a couple centuries," Jim added. Axl never got used to Jim's vast knowledge of everything. He seemed an unlikely genius: a lonely rancher in another nameless village in Idaho. A question reoccurred to Axl—a question he'd had every summer but had always been too timid to ask. Axl had been afraid of seeming intrusive or condescending. But now, sitting on the roof of Jim's ranch house, sharing a level of friendship only achieved in family, Axl said, "Uncle Jim, can I ask you a question?"

"Shoot."

"Well, I like Mackenzie fine—I mean, it's a super cool place and I love coming here every summer—and your ranch is great, but it's just…"

"Just what, son?"

Axl struggled to maintain eye contact. He failed. "I mean, you're really smart and you seem to be good at everything. So why did you decide to live out here in the middle of nowhere and run a ranch? I mean, no offense, but this seems like the kind of place where dreams go to die and people go to be forgotten."

Uncle Jim raised his eyebrows. Whatever shock he felt was masterfully muted by his expression. He diverted his gaze contemplatively and thought for a moment, scratching Brodie behind the ears. Uncle Jim smiled and said, "Well, I guess that depends on what your dreams are and who you want to be remembered by."

The two were quiet for a long time. The answer had been less of a justification than he'd expected. It had never occurred to Axl that not everybody in the world dreamt of being rich and famous—Axl sure did. "What about you?" Axl finally asked, "What are your dreams?"

"Not far from reality: be my own boss. Own my own land. Spend a lot of time around horses. I went to college—that was on the list. And getting married, that was on the list too."

Axl had never known Aunt Jess. She'd passed away pretty early on in her marriage to Jim; Axl couldn't remember how she'd died. Jim had had a long time to heal and wasn't sensitive about it, but Axl was gun-shy about bringing her up nonetheless. Now he worried he'd sobered their rooftop adventure beyond repair. "I'm sorry about Aunt Jess," Axl told Jim, "Dad says she was a really great lady."

"She was," Jim confirmed, "and anyone would've told you the same thing. When you ask about wanting to be remembered, Axl, all you have to do is think about people like Jess. Now, she wasn't anything close to famous—never had her name in lights or anything like that. People who didn't know her well probably wouldn't even call her pretty.

"But she had a heart as big as anything. There just wasn't a mean bone in her body and nobody had anything bad to say about her. She loved telling you why she liked you. I think *her* dream was to give someone a reason to smile every day. See, the way she made a difference in the world was one person at a time, and that's every bit as noble as anybody with a fan club or a yacht. So when she's remembered, she's remembered by friends only, because those were the only people she knew."

Axl smiled. Jim smiled back. The boy felt like he understood his uncle a lot better now. "So you have no regrets, then?" Axl asked.

Jim thought again. "Well, having kids would've been nice," he admitted, casting a casual glance at the stars above. "That was the one dream that didn't come true for either of us. But Jess said we'd keep trying even after the doctor told us it wasn't gonna happen. She died not too long after that."

An explosive popping noise interjected, illuminating the scene in a fleeting flash of pink. Somewhere far beyond the jagged black backdrop of trees, the firemen started lighting off aerials in the schoolyard. Axl wondered if clapping and cheering would be irreverent, given the conversation. It was Brodie who finally ended the awkwardness, barking with excitement. Jim and Axl joined him, hooting in celebration of America's independence.

CHAPTER THREE

AUTOMATON

A few mountains northeast of Atlas Ranch there was a clearing in the woods concealed by a near-perfect circle of conifers. It was so far off the beaten path that it was almost impossible to find if not by accident. It was the perfect place to keep a secret. It was here that the aliens first contacted Stanley Hobbes.

Stanley was returning to the spot now, compelled by the same mysterious force that had guided him so many times before. His summons came the typical way: the strange voice entered his mind unexpectedly that morning and told him to be in the clearing just after midnight. The hike took most of the afternoon and all of the evening, and for its duration, Stanley replayed the telepathic message over and over again in his mind. It was a strange gravelly voice, one which he both honored and feared, and its recent message had consumed him for weeks: *"If you knew it would save the world, would you leave the world behind?"*

Stanley entered the clearing timidly, at first seeing nothing. He stood half-crouching at its edge, breathing labored shallow breaths and keeping his big round eyes unblinking. He had no way of summoning the telepathic voice, so he waited vigilantly for something to happen. He waited for nearly thirty minutes. The whole time he stayed so still with his gaze fixed on the center of the clearing that not even the herd of mule deer that arrived there to feed detected him.

When the ship came, it came without fanfare, as always. It was almost completely soundless. The monotonous hum could've been drowned out by a whisper. Anyone less vigilant than the man at the clearing's edge might even have missed the ship's appearance at first. The mechanism of its invisibility slowly retracted, revealing the triangular craft so gradually that it had completely landed before the herd of deer noticed it and ran away. Stanley kept partly crouched and approached warily.

It was nearly two hundred feet tall and half as wide at the base, having no competition for height other than nearby mountains. It remained secret only by virtue of the density of the forest and the remoteness of this clearing. There wasn't a house for miles in any direction.

The cosmic steeple was covered in a mirrored exoskeleton that reflected the dark panorama of trees and the darker sky. Stanley watched himself draw closer to it in one of the flat mirrored faces, his fear magnified by his own hideously gaunt visage staring back at him. He was a man, though his build made him look more like a large emaciated child. His hands hung limply by their wrists, making his long thin fingers look heavy and cumbersome. Black shadows were pooled up in his hollow cheeks and eye sockets. His lips hung loosely open, showing the edges of crooked teeth. In this light he looked to himself almost as alien as the spaceship.

He kept a distance of at least thirty feet. He dared not get closer, no matter how long he had to wait. Without warning the ship released a spiteful hiss, shooting streams of misty vapor into the air. When the streams ran out there was another pause to endure. It ended with a blinding explosion of light so sudden that Stanley couldn't prepare for it, so brilliant that it knocked him off his feet, and just brief enough that it attracted no other attention. In less than ten seconds the display was over.

When Stanley, blinking, regained his vision, he saw the nameless being with the telepathic voice standing at the base of the ship, slowly closing the distance between them. Stanley had seen the alien many times but had never grown used to it. It was nearly seven feet tall and covered in mirrored plating like the ship.

The voice entered the man's mind again. *"Thank you for coming, Stanley Hobbes,"* the voice said.

Stanley started to reply but was startled by the loudness of his own voice. He started again, cautiously and submissively. He was always careful to sound as polite and friendly as he could—not because the nameless being had ever hurt him, but because he was sure that it could if it wanted to. "You're welcome," Stanley said. He took a long pause. "What do you want me to do?"

"I want you to make a decision," the alien answered.

Stanley knew what the alien wanted him to say. He was too frightened to refuse overtly. "A-about what?" he finally asked.

The alien paused for a long moment of thought. Then the voice in his mind repeated its question: *"Stanley, if you knew it would save the world, would you leave the world behind?"*

Stanley's brow furrowed. He hoped he'd misunderstood the invitation all along, but he knew he hadn't. "What do you mean?"

The alien chose its words carefully and tried to be clear. *"My ship has been away from Kalaxzos for a long time and needs maintenance. I won't be able to visit you again for at least two years. If you came back to my planet with me now we could continue our research. You could help a lot of people, even save lives."* Stanley was shaken. He swallowed hard. *"It's up to you,"* the alien added.

Stanley considered it for a long time. These secret midnight rendezvouses were frightening enough; he couldn't imagine a life where they never ended, no matter how much good it did. Still, he didn't want to disappoint the otherworldly being.

"Very well," the alien said suddenly, considering him with the dull red glow of his visor. It had read his thoughts, but it hadn't needed to. Stanley's apprehension was evident enough. In their previous interviews and encounters the being had often spoken of the great work being done on Kalaxzos and the brave, selfless volunteers who had given up their lives on Earth to support it. Stanley wasn't so obtuse that he hadn't anticipated the invitation, but he had avoided the topic. The alien had hoped for a different response but he didn't argue with Stanley's decision.

"What progress have you made on your test?" the voice finally asked, seeming to change the subject.

"Don't you already know?" Stanley asked with a tone of confusion, rubbing the scar on the back of his neck where he'd let the alien and his companions insert a microchip.

"Yes," the alien said, *"but a computer can only tell me so much. I can learn more from you. How do you feel?"*

Stanley thought for a moment. "Well, I don't smoke anymore," he said, "so it's working."

"Have your seizures lessened?"

"Yeah, a little bit."

The nameless being was silent for a moment. Stanley knew that the aliens could confirm or deny any physiological questions by reading the chip. He wondered if the silence confirmed or denied that his seizures had gone down.

"Are you happy, Stanley?" the alien asked.

The question was confusing. "What do you mean by that?"

"Is your life better than it was before?"

Stanley thought. "Yeah, I think so."

Though his helmet-like face was expressionless, the alien seemed to be concealing its feelings about the interview. Stanley just felt relieved to have moved past the question of leaving Earth. *"You have made commendable progress, Stanley Hobbes. You should be proud of yourself. Just remember to do all that I've taught you and you will continue to enjoy success."*

The nameless being turned and began to walk back to the ship, crushing tall grasses and thistles with its heavy metallic feet. It paused for a moment more before boarding, casting back to give Stanley one last glimpse of its luminous visor. *"And remember, Stanley: we will always be reading your chip. We're only here to help you."* Another blast of light, another hiss, and the ship rose off the ground, disappearing from sight as it ascended.

CHAPTER FOUR
RUMOR OF THE YEAR

Rumors rarely undersell reality. In fact, rumors tend to be the most exaggerated version of the story. Rumor is a forum where absurd conclusions are given undue credence for the sake of entertainment; at least, that was the case in Mackenzie. In such a laidback town, it was almost too easy to exaggerate anything that happened. The standard for excitement was comfortably low, which seemed to suit the storytellers: it provided them with uniquely fertile soil.

One of the most enduring rumors Mackenzie ever entertained was started the next day, on July 5th. The story was that Antonia LeBlanc—Olympian, actress, and America's premier mixed martial artist—had been seen eating breakfast at a restaurant in Mackenzie. Different versions of the story disagreed on which of Mackenzie's five restaurants she'd eaten at, as well as the exact date it took place. Some locals reported interacting with her or seeing her around town on a number of days that week. Were it true, she would have been the most distinguished guest Mackenzie had ever hosted. But even many of those who disseminated the story doubted that Antonia "Madame Guillotine" LeBlanc had really even heard of Mackenzie, Idaho.

Later that year she appeared in an action movie in which a few of her scenes were filmed in McCall, a town just over an hour north of Mackenzie. This fueled the rumors as well as sparked newer, more sensational ones: had she been scouting Mackenzie as a future shooting location? If she'd been seen on several different days she must have been very taken with the town. Whom had she met? Did she think they would be good in movies? Where had she stayed? Was she involved with somebody in town? Might there be a scandal?

In its remarkably long tenure, the rumor introduced new vitality into the town—a buzz of anticipation that provided excitement almost as great as the fruition of any of the theories surrounding it. Indeed, that whole year was defined by that rumor alone. But as thrilling as it was, the Rumor of the Year could never have approached the strange and fantastic truth. In this single case, the rumor undersold reality.

For the record, many aspects of the rumors were true. For the record, the restaurant that Antonia LeBlanc ate at was Hometown Inn. Every morning of Axl's summertime visits started with eating breakfast there. It was a small place with no remarkable characteristics: wood siding, faded red roof, just one story. The table nearest the door was always home to a 1,000-piece puzzle in progress that patrons could work on at their leisure when they came in. When somebody couldn't find Jim at home that's usually where they looked first.

"New puzzle," Axl observed as they took their seats that Thursday morning. Uncle Jim mumbled an affirmative. He seemed a little disappointed that somebody else had completed the previous puzzle. They studied the picture of a carnival depicted on the box.

"Reminds me of *Meet Me in St. Louis*," Uncle Jim said. Axl agreed, though he'd never seen the movie.

Half-heartedly Axl helped Uncle Jim organize the pieces into little islands of similar color. They all seemed the same dull blurry reds and yellows. Axl stifled a sigh and wondered if Jim could see through his façade of interest. He let his mind wander as his eyes toured the familiar rustic decorations on the walls: antique-looking signs, "snake oil" ads, rusty coils of barbed while, mounted animal heads. He rubbed a puzzle piece between his thumb and forefinger unconsciously.

The breakfast crowd wasn't big that morning. Three other patrons sat alone. There was a haggard-looking girl sitting at a table near the kitchen door counting the money in her wallet. She kept it partly concealed in a lumpy backpack sitting in her lap, but it was clear what she was doing. Her backpack was covered in doodles she'd done with sharpies and gel pens, as were her worn-out Converse shoes. She was medium-built but was wearing a baggy hoodie that gave her the shape of a lawn gnome. The tattered sweatshirt bore an NFL team emblem that was so faded that it was almost unrecognizable. Axl guessed she was probably sixteen or seventeen.

At a table near a window sat a woman with a face and skin that made her look like a vacuum-sealed bag. She'd ordered a small breakfast which she'd hardly touched and now looked aimlessly out the window. The window might have been a dried-up wishing well with no pennies in it. She leaned her head against it wearily, pale morning light accenting the recesses of her boney face. With the washed-out tones of her skin and short-cropped hair along with her despondent expression, she could have been the model for the saddest picture ever painted.

The third patron sat in the far corner of the room busily organizing her life on her phone. She had a decidedly athletic build and the darkest skin Axl had ever seen. She dressed in a style that spoke both of her affluence and of her fitness. Her coarse black hair was held tightly back in cornrows that made Axl identify her almost immediately.

"Uncle Jim!" Axl exclaimed suddenly. "Do you know who that is?"

Uncle Jim's eyes followed Axl's finger to the table in the corner of the room where the woman sat. Axl didn't wait for Jim to answer: "That's Antonia LeBlanc!"

"Who?"

"Oh come on!" Axl whispered, not quietly. "She was in the Olympics! And the UFC! And the movies!"

Uncle Jim eyed her discreetly. He had no idea who Antonia LeBlanc was, but still said with a tone of skeptic dismissal, "Huh. She does look a bit like her." He returned to island-making.

"It *is* her!" Axl insisted with frustration in his voice, "How would you know? You don't even watch TV." This wasn't entirely true; Uncle Jim *did* watch some television. But as far as Axl was concerned anything that came out before digital high-definition didn't count as "TV."

"Maybe you should talk to her," Jim offered. Axl didn't respond, mortified by the idea of approaching someone so famous. The woman suddenly looked up from her phone and winked at him conspicuously.

Axl's ears glowed pink. He cautiously scanned the dining room, hoping people weren't staring at him. The haggard girl near the kitchen door scratched her head, still staring into her lap. The thin woman by the window was having a whispered exchange with a man who'd just arrived at the diner. Axl had seen the man before but didn't know him. With comical thick lips and buggy eyes he had a face like a caricature. He conducted himself awkwardly, not sitting down and keeping his hands in his pockets, all the while with a smile of feigned confidence spread across his face. Neither he nor the thin woman nor the girl seemed to notice Axl.

The dark woman in the corner still stared at the boy and raised her eyebrows welcomingly. Axl noisily scooted out from the table and walked across the dining room.

"Hey, are you Antonia LeBlanc?" he asked, his voice cracking a little.

"Yeah, that's me," she answered pleasantly. "What's your name?"

The boy grinned like a cherub. "I'm Axl," he told her. Antonia cast a glance back to the boy's table where the older man sat. "Oh, and that's my uncle Jim," he added. Uncle Jim appraised them with a casual wave. "I saw you in *Megabulldozer Apocalypse III*," Axl told her. "You were great!"

She laughed. "I just did what I do best."

"Well it was awesome! You were seriously like the coolest part!"

"Well, thank you so much, Axl," Antonia smiled, then asked with a tone of surprise, "Your uncle lets you watch the *Megabulldozer* movies?"

Axl's ears glowed brighter. "I went with a friend," he answered sheepishly. "It's okay, I'm fourteen."

"Do you ever get told you look young for your age?" Antonia laughed.

"All the time!" Axl replied, rolling his eyes. Guesses in the past year had been as low as nine years old.

Antonia laughed again. She was a genuine and likable kind of person; people on TV always said that about her. Everything about her demanded attention: the vibrant, personable way she conducted herself; her imposing athletic build; the exotic features of her triangular face. In this modest setting she stood out like forest fire.

"What the heck are you doing in a place like Mackenzie?" Axl asked.

"Passing through," she answered.

"Figures," Axl said. "Passing through is just about all there is to do around here."

Chuck Hocum owned the restaurant. He came out of the kitchen and started setting burdened plates on Jim's table. Jim was pretty good friends with Chuck, as were most people who had met Chuck. "You know who that lady is?" Jim asked Chuck casually.

Chuck cast a quick glance at her. "Hmm...out-of-towner. She looks familiar; is she famous?"

"She must be," Jim said, "Axl's been yapping about her ever since we sat down. Antonia LeBlanc?"

"You know what?" Chuck said, scratching his short prickly beard, "I think she's some athlete or something. Is Axl into sports?"

Jim started with the hash browns. "Axl's into a little bit of everything."

Chuck gave an overindulgent laugh and dismissed himself back to the kitchen. He seemed to be in an uncharacteristic rush that morning, darting around the room and in and out of the kitchen. It was a change of pace that made him seem almost anxious. Of course he maintained his normal cheery demeanor—his face was trapped in a perpetual grin—but regulars like Jim knew better. "You running the show by yourself this morning?" Jim asked as Chuck passed by again.

"No, I got help: Me, Myself, and I," Chuck smiled, waited for a laugh, and then explained, "My waitress asked for the morning off and I told her okay, but then my wife felt sick this morning so she's sleeping in."

Jim raised his eyebrows. "Sorry to hear that about your wife. Hope she's better by lunch."

"Well that makes two of us—but sleeping in sure sounds nice, doesn't it? Heck, *I* ought to get pregnant one of these days!"

Jim chuckled. "When is that baby due, by the way?"

"Not soon enough." Chuck answered proudly, a big jolly grin spreading wider across his face. "It's gonna be a girl, did I tell you that?"

Jim nodded. "Thought of a name yet?"

"Well, my wife doesn't think much of 'Chuck Junior,'" Chuck joked. "Maybe she'll let me name her after you."

Jim chuckled dismissively. "Yeah. Right."

Chuck eyed Jim's chicken-fried steak. It'd sat for a minute, he hoped it was warm enough. "How's the ranch coming?" Chuck asked conversationally, checking his watch discreetly.

"Only a day or two behind schedule," Jim answered, "which is really impressive considering what little help that kid is. He's a really good boy and I like the heck out of him, but he doesn't seem to know how to use his hands. City living. I'll tell you who's a huge help, though: have I told you about my guy Juan?"

"Maybe so. Who is he?"

"Only the best thing in construction. He's trying to go into business for himself—building up from smaller, slower projects like mine. You should hire him to build an addition onto the restaurant. He's not expensive—not yet. I'll tell you what, though, when he's through with my place everybody's gonna want him!"

"Might have to look into him," Chuck said politely, if insincerely. Jim's means were not Chuck's.

The bell above the door chimed. Stanley Hobbes entered with an unknowing grin.

CHAPTER FIVE

BEAKER

I said that I know much of what I do about the Experiments only secondhand. This part of the Mackenzie Experiments is one such case. I was only a baby that summer and my family had not yet moved to Mackenzie. I don't doubt that Hometown Inn contributed to the welcoming small-town feel that inspired my parents to move there later that year. The Inn was just before the traffic light on the left; it was easy enough to miss.

Like most businesses in Mackenzie it had changed hands and names a number of times. Chuck and Julie Hocum had been running the restaurant for only a couple of years and had redubbed it "Hometown Inn." It was a hopeful name: words like "inn" generally imply lodging and, though the Hocum's little restaurant wasn't set up for boarders, they had a goal of turning it into a bed-and-breakfast. Who could have guessed that this undistinguished business in Mackenzie, Idaho would be the site of what happened that day? Who could have guessed that at the center of it would be a person as unlikely as Stanley Hobbes?

Nobody was ever a hundred percent sure what was wrong with Stanley. He had a lot of problems, no argument. He had something like a mixture of autism, epilepsy, and paranoia. The paranoia was a recent development. He graduated high school at twenty years old and now, at just a few years shy of thirty, he was still living on a farm just outside of Mackenzie with his father. It suited him. Most of his friends were still local, and most of his days were filled with walking around town visiting them.

Stanley's height was average, his build was small, and his demeanor made him seem a decade-and-a-half younger than he really was. He had excited-looking eyes, one pale gray and one blue, set deeply in a strange narrow face with a mass of red hair atop it that was all one irreconcilable cowlick. Everyone called him "Beaker," like the *Muppet Show* character.

The first stop of Stanley's day was usually Hometown Inn to visit Chuck Hocum. Chuck had a disposition that inclined him to becoming friends with just about everyone. He was an authentic, friendly, humble man with a wide, smiling face and stocky build that made him seem the embodiment of a much younger Santa Claus. More than that, though, he had a certain presence about him—a carefree and neighborly countenance that put you right at ease. That morning the absence of Mrs. Hocum and the usual waitress had put Chuck noticeably closer to the edge, but he compensated tactfully with his winning grin and incessant joking.

"What's up, Pal?" Stanley greeted his friend loudly. "Pal" was Stanley's nickname for everyone, even strangers.

"Gas prices, ceilings, and the planet Mars," Chuck replied with a fleeting, but sincere-looking grin.

"How's the wife and kids?" Stanley asked mechanically. This follow-up question was Stanley's go-to, especially when the person wasn't married and had no children. He always expected a laugh but rarely got one.

"Oh they're good, Beaker," Chuck answered, "real good." Chuck disappeared into the kitchen. Stanley stood for a moment in confusion before timidly following him.

Stanley watched as Chuck hustled around the kitchen doing this and that. Chuck could sense Stanley's discomfort, so he forced another smile. "How are you this fine Fifth of July, Beaker?"

"I'm good," Stanley said. "Where's Julie?"

"She's sick with the baby this morning so I'm handling breakfast on my own, that's all. Sorry if I seem a little distracted."

"Can't Becky help?"

"Well, Becky was going to get home late last night so she asked if she could have this morning off. She said she'll come in as soon as she gets up. It should be fine, there aren't too many people out there…you don't think I'm too much of a pushover, do you? I mean as a boss."

"No." Stanley toyed with the corner of the drawer. Then he asked in a sincere tone, "Can I help?"

Chuck considered it for a moment. A long moment. "I dunno, Stanley. How'd you sleep last night?"

"Good." Stanley lied.

"And how's your smoking?"

"I haven't smoked in months!" Stanley announced proudly.

Chuck thought a moment more, smiled cautiously, and said, "That'd be great Stanley. You can help until Julie or Becky comes in. Sound good?"

Stanley nodded excitedly, tying on an apron. His enthusiasm was full to the brim. The only thing he'd ever had resembling a job was helping his dad out on the family farm, but he was too clumsy to be trusted with most farmyard tasks. A wait staff position was a big deal to Stanley. Chuck handed Stanley a large and a small plate and opened the door slightly. "Ok, Beak, you see that table in the corner where that woman is talking to Axl?"

"The black lady?"

"Yep, that's her" Chuck answered. "These plates are for that woman. Understand?"

"I understand, yeah," Stanley nodded enthusiastically. Chuck wore a proud grin and motioned for Stanley to go ahead. Stanley pushed the swinging door open with his shoulder.

"You helping out this morning, Beaker?" Jim asked when he saw Stanley enter with the plates. This morning he was too focused on his assignment to even notice Jim's question.

He stepped around Axl without introduction, setting the plates in front of Antonia. "This is what you ordered, right?" Stanley asked, interrupting the conversation.

"Yes, thank you," she smiled and then finished her sentence.

"Beaker!" Jim said again, getting Stanley's attention. "You helping out this morning?"

"Yeah," Stanley answered, "Chuck said I could."

"Well you look like you belong," Jim complimented. "Keep up the good work, Beaker."

"Thanks!" Stanley beamed, turning back toward the kitchen. Jim chuckled as Stanley walked away.

The gnomish-looking girl grabbed Stanley's shirt as he passed her table. "Hey!" she scolded, "Turn around! I'm trying to talk to you." Stanley spun around, startled. "Did the world run out of French toast in the past twenty minutes?" she demanded irritably.

"Sorry, ma'am," Stanley said sheepishly, "I'll go ask Chuck."

"Yeah, why don't you go ask Chuck?" she repeated mockingly, then muttered, "...sucky service, understaffed, drafty…"

What happened next happened almost all at once. The door's bell chimed as the thin woman walked out, leaving the thick-lipped cartoon man sitting alone at her table. Stanley reentered the dining room a moment later, making an obvious arc to avoid the disagreeable girl's table. Stanley set a mug on Jim's table then burned his shaking hands while pouring. The coffee pot shattered around Stanley's feet when it hit the floor. "Nice!" the girl called out insultingly as Stanley darted out of the room. He stumbled through the kitchen, shoving Chuck with a limp flailing arm. He fell whirling out the back door and collapsed in a convulsing heap on the ground.

How does one describe astral displacement? Even after all I've seen a learned it still seems so abstract. In some realm coexisting with the physical world, there is an astral one in which our mortal bodies have counterparts. These metaphysical bodies exist co-dependently with their physical forms and encompass all the immaterial elements of identity and self; most people call them "souls."

Seconds after Stanley ran from the room, the metaphysical world experienced a massive localized upheaval, and the souls of six strangers switched places.

CHAPTER SIX
DISPLACEMENT

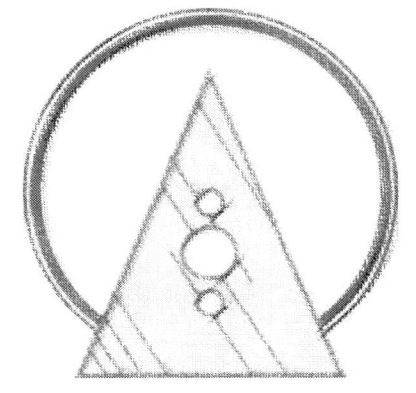

Phoebe let out a scream to rival a drum major's whistle. She had never felt anything like it. Fear, confusion, weightlessness. Disorientation, dizziness, unknowing—something like what babies must feel when they're first brought out of the womb. Sinking in reverse. A buzzing, numbing lightheadedness, but all over. A total separation from reality for seconds that felt like minutes. And then it was gone.

And when it was gone, Phoebe could see herself stumble clumsily out of her chair on the other side of the room. She did the only thing she could think of to do: she ran. She kicked her chair over as she forced away from the table, she pushed past the little boy who stood in her way, she flung the door open with barely even touching the handle and shrieked when she saw that the reflection in the windows of cars outside was not her own. She turned and ran. She ran like she'd run so many times before, each step taking her farther and farther away from home. And like so many times before, she ran without reservation or thought, operating on reckless instinct and the will to survive.

Jim's reaction was perhaps the most surprising of all. After a moment of trance-like confusion and a feeling like his brain was being thrown across the room like a baseball, his conscious settled into Axl's head. Phoebe, inhabiting Antonia's muscular frame, nearly knocked him over when she shoved past him. He turned hastily and saw her burst out the door. Around the room there were shouts of dismay and awkward attempts at locomotion. Half-formed judgement drove Jim across the room where he blocked the exit with the small fourteen-year-old body he now possessed.

He watched the chaos for a moment. Jim's own former self sat transfixed at his table, over and over again asking what had just happened. With each repetition the voice grew more and more shrill and tight until it became almost unintelligible. Anxious tears formed in the eyes.

The thick-lipped man rose hastily to his feet. He faltered, his knees buckled, and he collapsed back into his chair. His face made a terrible montage of every awful expression it knew before settling on one of confounded shock.

The haggard teenager approached Jim hastily, somewhat hysterical. "This is not me!" she asserted with panic in her voice. "I just ran out of here. Where did I go? Get out of the way!"

Jim didn't answer, cautiously peering out the window behind him. In the parking lot the thin woman was draped haphazardly across the hood of her car like a bird that had hit a window, writhing and gasping. Jim drew a terrified breath, turned back, and watched his former body's face twist perplexedly as it considered him. The face breathed laboriously, muttering and wheezing as tears streamed from its startled-looking eyes.

A steady moan of disturbed disarray seeped from the thick-lipped man.

"I'm getting away!" the teenage girl said anxiously, "Please! Please can I get out of here! Let me out!"

Jim endured the panic for fifteen overwhelming seconds more as his mind raced. Finally he shouted in his pubescent voice, "Shut up! Everybody shut up! Just be quiet!" Weeping and whimpers were subdued as all eyes fell on Jim. "Calm down," he implored, "we need to figure this out." He thought for moment.

Chuck, or so it seemed, entered from the kitchen.

"Chuck—" Jim began.

"Who, me?" he interrupted. "I'm not Chuck."

This revelation was almost too much for Jim to endure. He fought his inner hysteria. "Just...everybody stay calm, okay? Does anybody have any idea what just happened?" Around the room voices sounded off negative responses. Each person seemed unsettled by his or her own unfamiliar voice. The former Jim whimpered and grunted as he noisily cleared his throat, trying to subdue his emotions. Jim spoke over it. "For now I think the best thing for us to do is not to lose sight of each other, so let's just stay put."

"I can't stay put!" the haggard girl objected. "I already left!"

"Who are you?" Jim asked.

"I'm Antonia LeBlanc!" she exclaimed. Jim's head hurt already and the confusion had barely started. Former Jim whimpered.

"So who is Chuck right now?" Jim asked.

The thick-lipped man arose. "I'm Chuck, Jim."

A few voices started to rise. Jim threw his hands up. "Hold it! Hold it." He made eye contact with each of them in turn, shuddering slightly when making eye contact with the face he'd seen only in mirrors for the past sixty years. "Let's keep this organized or we'll never figure it out. Let's go one at a time and say who we are, okay?"

The others nodded hesitantly.

They waited for an awkward moment. Jim had taken charge and was the most level-headed at that point, but the surreal trauma of the situation was making his thought process start and stall like a student driver. Jim finally said, "Okay, I guess I'll start. My name is Jim Boyd." He pointed to his former self, still seated at the table. "I'm a rancher who lives near here." It was funny in a way, the scrawny fourteen-year-old with a mouth full of braces claiming to be the gray old farmer. But whatever potential the scene had for humor was lost in the helpless horror each of them felt. "I can already tell you that I've somehow got my brain into the head of my nephew Axl."

Jim was interrupted when somebody tried to open the door his back was pressed against. He turned only enough to grab the corner of the "open" sign hanging in the window and flip it over to the "closed" side. Chuck let out a sigh through his nose: the person Jim had just shut out was one of the regulars. Unexpected closures were bad for business and friendships. Jim waited for the person to leave and then nodded toward the man who used to be Chuck, prompting his introduction.

The man was cautious, unblinking. He seemed distrustful of the strangers—totally unlike the real Chuck. The heavyset cook had traded his grin for loose lips forming a small lopsided O. It contracted into a fearful and melancholy expression. He took a defensive half-step backwards, saying, "I don't know that I should tell you who I am."

"That's fair," Jim said judiciously. "What can we call you?"

He paused, thought, and said, "Dale." He gestured toward his former self, the thick-lipped man seated at a nearby table. With his shocked expression the man looked even more like a cartoon character than before. Jim saw a resemblance between the way the strange man had carried himself before and the way that "Chuck" looked now. Dale had worn the same expression after being left alone at the table. Jim suddenly remembered the thin woman who'd been sitting with Dale but, turning, he found that she and her car had disappeared from the parking lot.

"Who was that woman you were with?" Jim asked Dale.

"Beats me," Dale answered. "I was just being friendly. She never gave me her name."

Jim frowned. "Well, whoever she was, she's gone now." He nodded toward the thick-lipped cartoon man. "So you're Chuck…" Then finally he addressed his former self: "…and you're Axl." Both affirmed gravely. Jim ran through the transfers in his mind, trying to keep all of this perplexing new information in order. The prodigious memory he'd been endowed with had never seemed such a great asset as it did now.

"Did anybody know this girl?" he asked, pointing to the teenager who'd identified herself as Antonia. No positive replies. "Well, she's got Antonia for the time being and Antonia has her."

Antonia swore anxiously. "I'm supposed to be meeting with my agent in two hours in McCall! What am I supposed to do?"

"Agent?" Jim asked.

"A movie," she explained, "I'm supposed to shoot some scenes for a movie. You think they want me to show up on set like *this*?"

Another person came to the door, peering inside and rapping on the glass. Jim stayed pressed up against it, but turned and pointed at the sign.

"Jim," Chuck explained, "that's Becky, my waitress."

The young boy, or so he seemed, furrowed his brows and thought, his eyes narrow. He looked right at Dale. "Here," Jim said, "you're Chuck now; tell her to take the day off."

"Me?" The others stared at him. Jim stepped aside, offering Dale the door as he held it closed. Dale approached it haltingly, casting back at each of them as if suspecting they were all in on the same practical joke. Swallowing hard, he opened the door a crack and said unconvincingly, "Look, there's been a family emergency so we're gonna have to close for the day. Just come back tomorrow, okay?" The girl seemed confused but didn't argue. Dale could pass for Chuck in appearance only; the imposter was exposed through every mannerism and pattern of speech.

Jim watched the girl leave out of the corner of his eye, resuming his defense of the exit. "Anybody else think this place is maybe a little too public?" Nobody answered for a moment.

"What are you getting at?" Dale asked.

"Just that it might not be a bad idea to move this crisis to my ranch." Immediately remarks of disagreement broke out.

"We should just stay here! This is where it happened, maybe it'll happen again."

"For how long? Now look, Jim, I need the restaurant to be open today."

"I'm sure you're a very good man, but I really have to go now!"

Jim fought to keep his head. Behind him a small family of out-of-towners approached the door and read the sign, peering curiously inside at all the animated people arguing. Chuck released a despondent sigh as they turned and left. There had been eight of them.

"Ok!" Chuck finally interjected. "I'm with Jim, it's too public." The others listened. "If only for the sake of my business I think it's a good idea to go to Jim's ranch. I know Jim real well, he's a good man. We can figure this thing out there."

The wait for responses was a long one. Brains strained for explanations and options. Finally Axl, who had been holding his head in his arms the whole time, looked up with tear-stained eyes and whimpered "Ok."

Dale sighed, then gave a half-hearted consent. "What a zoo," he muttered.

"Ok," Antonia finally said, "Now can I leave?"

CHAPTER SEVEN
THE RUNAWAY

Phoebe was less than a mile down the road hiding in a convenience store bathroom, trying to reconcile the strange, frightening dream that had become her reality. It was a single-user restroom, and Phoebe was grateful: she'd never felt a greater need for privacy. She spent nearly thirty minutes there, the first half of which were spent curled up in the farthest corner from the door, as if trying to keep away from some animal that had her trapped. She covered her face, tears of fright quietly weeping forth as she breathed heavily into her hands. Occasionally she'd uncover her eyes, hoping not to see that unfamiliar bathroom with that unfamiliar woman staring back in the full-length mirror. Occasionally she'd rub her muscular arms and legs vigorously as if trying to wipe the body off of her, but to no avail.

The terror gradually subsided, Phoebe composed herself and slowly she arose, approaching the mirror cautiously. She examined her new form, curiosity and excitement slowly taking the place of fear and confusion. It seemed every sensation of this body was different from her own. She was uncommonly tall and strong for a woman—

especially strong. Her dark skin felt tense and hard all over. Her hair was coarse but shiny, its deep onyx blackness contrasted by a vibrantly-colored headband. Phoebe smeared the makeup she'd spoiled while crying, trying to make the face look more like it did when she'd noticed the woman in the restaurant that morning.

In her exodus from Hometown Inn Phoebe had instinctively grabbed the wallet sitting on the table near her hand. She'd been intending to grab the backpack she'd been living out of, but in its absence the wallet sufficed. She picked it up from where it now sat on the bathroom floor, exploring its contents. She'd never seen such a variety of cards in one wallet. She finally came across a driver's license. "Antonia LeBlanc." Who was Antonia LeBlanc?

A knock came at the door. "Excuse me?" the store attendant interrupted, "Are you okay in there? We've got somebody else who needs to use the restroom."

Phoebe closed the wallet, released an irritated sigh through her nose, and opened the door. The attendant looked at her apologetically, noting the redness of her eyes. "Sorry," he apologized, "is everything alright?"

"Yeah, I'm fine," she said dismissively, pushing past him. She drifted toward the exit but stopped abruptly, not wanting to leave the relative security she felt in the store. She began exploring the few aisles of goods available, remembering that she'd missed breakfast. Her new body didn't feel hungry, yet in her mind she was still dissatisfied. She ran her thumb along the wallet in her hand, wondering how much Antonia LeBlanc could afford in snacks. She was dressed well, Phoebe considered, and the expensive-looking car she'd seen in front of Hometown Inn might have been hers. She collected an assortment of easy snacks: jerky, M&M's, a soda, and a tube of chips. She laid them beside the cash register.

"Will that be everything?" the attendant asked routinely from behind the register.

"Do you assume I've forgotten something?" Phoebe asked sharply. The attendant averted his eyes in embarrassment.

Just as Phoebe was getting a credit card out of the wallet she felt a hand on her back. Turning frantically she came face-to-face with her own former self. "What are you doing?" Antonia demanded accusingly.

"Nothing." Phoebe replied, making for the door. Antonia followed.

"Hey!" the attendant called after Phoebe, "Aren't you Antonia LeBlanc?"

"Oh, no," Phoebe called back sarcastically, "you've got me confused with some other five-foot-nine, 145-pound Amazon!"

Antonia waited until she and Phoebe were outside to confront her. "Are you kidding me?" Antonia interrogated in a harsh whisper. "You're me for twenty minutes and you're going to just start spending my money? Who the heck do you think you are?"

"Antonia LeBlanc apparently," Phoebe said, nodding toward the confused-looking attendant. He watched them curiously from inside the store.

"*I'm* Antonia LeBlanc," Antonia corrected. "Who are you?"

"Hold on," Phoebe interjected, "why does everybody keep acting like they know you?"

"I'm a champion MMA fighter," Antonia answered impatiently, "now who are you?"

Phoebe paused, processing this new information. "Jess," she answered. It was the false name Phoebe had been giving out for days.

"Jess what?"

"Just Jess."

Antonia sighed with frustration and prodded Phoebe toward her Porsche Spyder. "Girl, you are going to ruin my reputation with stuff like that back there. I always treat my fans with respect, alright?"

"For somebody who beats people up for a living you seem to care a lot about what people think of you."

"I'm an athlete, not a thug," Antonia recited in her defense, buckling her seatbelt. "And I do *not* weigh 145 pounds!"

Phoebe held out Antonia's wallet. "Your driver's license says you do."

Antonia accepted the wallet and set it in the center console. "Well, it's out of date," she rationalized.

Phoebe found her backpack sitting in the passenger's seat. She set it in her lap, checking the zippers. "You didn't go through my bag, did you?" she asked accusingly.

"Oh, please! What could I have possibly wanted in your backpack?" Antonia said, hiding her guilt with her irritated tone. She pulled back onto the main road.

A big gray Ford pickup idled on the side of the road. It pulled out ahead of them. Chuck was driving. It was Jim's truck and he would have driven it himself, but in the body of a fourteen-year-old he didn't want to risk getting pulled over.

"Where are we going?" Phoebe asked the fighter.

"We're following that truck," Antonia said. "Apparently this whole brain-transfer thing happened to everyone in that restaurant so we're going to some guy's ranch to try to figure out what to do."

"There you go, that's smart," Phoebe mocked, "here you are, totally helpless, so why not let a total stranger talk you into going to his house?"

"I'm a total stranger and you got in my car," Antonia countered. Phoebe shut up for an awkward thirty seconds. Antonia turned on the radio.

"What is this?" Phoebe asked, raising condescending eyebrows at the song.

"No." Antonia answered.

"No?"

"The song is called 'No.'"

"Interesting," Phoebe said. "I hate it."

"Are you for real?" Antonia shot back. "Are you always like this?"

"Like what?" came the defensive reply. Another pause.

Antonia sighed. "Do you have a mom you need me to call or something?"

"No." Phoebe said flatly. "And don't bring it up again."

Phoebe Rhodes had always wondered if she'd be good at running away from home. Now that she had, she wasn't sure what to measure it by. She'd imagined it would be something like wilderness survival. Admittedly, she knew even less about wilderness survival than she did about running away, but she figured that if she didn't feel desperate or scared it was probably because she knew what she was doing. But she had left her home in Oregon eight days prior and she was beginning to feel more and more desperate as her wallet became thinner and thinner. Still, her only goal had been to get as far away from home as possible and she'd been successful. Now she had no goals.

In the past week she'd only told two people that she was a runaway, and she'd since sworn off telling anyone else. The first time she told it she was looking for sympathy. The person listened to her story and scolded her for being reckless and self-centered. Phoebe had received a lecture about how good her life really was, followed by demands that she give the stranger her parents' telephone number. The second time she told her story she was looking for validation. The second person she told cut the story short and called the police. Phoebe had been doing a lot of running in those eight days.

She'd come to favor these little nothing towns: no cops. They seemed accustomed to hitch hikers, too, though people were suspicious when they asked where she was headed and she didn't have an answer. Phoebe was paranoid about using her phone, so she only ever turned it on to look up names of towns for people to drive her to.

Phoebe decided she was uniquely prone to getting picked up when thumbing a ride; she was totally unimposing. There wasn't a better word to describe Phoebe's appearance than "average." She was five-foot-four with a fair complexion, dark blond hair, blue eyes, and a face as plain as a wire hanger. Not ugly, just plain. She had turned seventeen recently, but she decided she'd have to try to pass for nineteen if she didn't want people turning her in. The story she told now was that she'd been driving home from college, that her car had broken down, and that she'd been walking for hours looking for a town. "Did you see my car on the side of the road a few miles back?" she'd say. They always admitted they'd missed it.

Running away from home had taught Phoebe that she was good at lying, but not at budgeting. What money she had was the few hundred dollars she'd been saving up for years—the "Car Fund" she called it. When her parents wouldn't help her buy one it became the "Runaway Fund." Now, just over a week later, the Runaway Fund was a fistful of one-dollar bills and a twenty.

The circumstances behind Phoebe's running away had been a lot more complicated than the disagreement over the car, but that was the fight that made "independence" seem worth it. She revisited the heated exchange with her parents several times every day in her memories. She stewed over it and others, her whole life reduced to a collection of times her parents had used the word "no" and times she'd used the word "hate." It was keeping her in a perpetual bitter mood that, if unintentionally, had become an integral part of her assumed persona.

In truth she didn't distrust Antonia, nor did she hold her apparent affluence against her—though she did hate rich people as a rule. Phoebe was actually comforted to be in the company of somebody who seemed as vulnerable as she was. If Antonia's approach hadn't been so harsh right off the bat then they might have become fast friends or at least comrades. But Phoebe was sick of being scolded, yelled at, and treated like a child. She was sick of people not empathizing with her and she was sick of being pushed around. The world seemed to be peopled entirely with controlling adults, so independence and vagrantism seemed to be Phoebe's only hope for happiness.

From the moment she'd woken up in a smelly hay barn to the moment she'd arrived in a yuppie sports car at a yuppie vacation ranch, Phoebe's thoughts had been black with contempt. The beauty of the Idaho landscape and the mildness of the summer morning had been lost to her as she sat in brooding silence all the way to Atlas Ranch. Her part in the contentious din that ensued between the strangers that day was by far the most cutting and profane. She'd always been sarcastic and a bit contentious, but there were certain words she would never have dared say, even if she thought them. Now the desperation, lack of sleep, and angry thoughts were finally drawing them out of her. Yet they were lost in a cloud of competing voices as the group of strangers deliberated what to do in Jim Boyd's front room.

CHAPTER EIGHT
CHARRETTE

There was seating enough for more than their number, but the only ones who sat were Chuck and Axl. The others had taken seats and had since risen with the volume of the conversation, save only Dale who hadn't sat down at all, as if fearing his seat would be booby trapped. Chuck and Axl were barely involved—by nature neither one of them were confrontational. Axl rarely shut up, but when he did it was usually in the presence of an argument. Besides, he was still embarrassed about crying at Hometown Inn and didn't want to attract attention to himself.

Now that Antonia had found Phoebe she advocated returning to Hometown Inn, hoping that the same impossible phenomenon would reoccur. Jim said they should stay out of the public eye until they were sure of what to do. In the form of Axl he'd dismissed all his hired help for the day as soon as they'd arrived at the ranch. They'd looked to Axl—in the form of Jim—for explanation but he offered none. Jim also had to dismiss Brodie, his border collie, to the porch for the duration of their meeting, as Dale had "this thing about dogs."

Dale, who still wasn't convinced this wasn't all a dream, was all for everybody going home and sleeping it off— "and if that doesn't work we'll call a doctor tomorrow morning," he said. The others tried their best to ignore his comments.

Chuck reached mechanically for the baseball cap he usually wore. He would use its bill to scratch his head, but when he found it missing he simply ran his hand through his hair. It was different from his old body's hair: Chuck's own ruddy brown hair was coarse and thick and unkempt. Dale's was much thinner but also longer, darker, and combed back neatly.

Chuck cast Axl a discreet glance, breathing a tense sigh through his nose. He kept forgetting that the thin old rancher now had a young boy for a brain, but Axl's mannerisms always reminded him: the sloppy posture, the inattentive wandering of the eyes, the incessant touching of the face. It was almost as strange as watching his own body being controlled by someone else. There was nobody in the group that Chuck was nearly as familiar with as Jim. He recognized Dale and had tried to be friendly in the past but had never gotten much talking out of him. Dale had to be the one person in Mackenzie that Chuck wasn't on a first-name basis with. The young girl Jess and the athlete Antonia were both new to him, and Chuck knew barely more about Axl than his name. He was in the company of strangers.

Chuck's mind was somewhere else. He was thinking of his wife, Julie, wondering what she was doing and if she was worried about him. He'd always said she'd do fine without him, but still he felt sick at the thought of her being alone, especially now that a baby was on the way. She never complained and she rarely asked for help, but he knew he'd feel no peace until he was with her again. He leaned forward as if to stand, waiting for the courage to get up and tell the angry group that he wanted to go home. It felt strange not having a beard to scratch or a big belly to rest his folded arms on.

The conversation derailed when, in the midst of the din, Phoebe turned to Dale and shouted, "Would you just shut up?! Nobody is listening to you anyway!" The others stopped abruptly. Dale was speechless.

True to form, it was Jim who took command. "Okay, let's all just calm down for a minute," he urged, putting his hands up. "We're all under a lot of pressure right now and losing our heads isn't going to fix anything. Let's just keep this civil and diplomatic, alright?"

They each slowed their breathing and nodded. Antonia whispered a "sorry." Phoebe didn't.

Jim ran a hand through his thick dark curly hair. His boyish face was more beautiful than it was handsome, even with the furrowed brow of frustration. He relaxed his face gradually, all except for his eyes, which he kept squinted. Jim had been squinting for so long in his old body that he couldn't give it up in his new one. It was important to Jim that everyone remembered who he really was. If he was going to assume leadership he needed more authority than was afforded by the visage of a fourteen-year-old, especially one with braces (which Jim was sure he'd never get used to). He knew the squint would help, as well as the drawl he spoke with. Lastly he'd decided to wear the black cowboy hat he was known for. It fit poorly but was successfully distinguishing. Axl had no qualms about relinquishing it; this whole experience was so stressful that he hadn't even realized that his dream of becoming his cowboy uncle had literally come true.

"With as little sense as our situation makes," Jim reasoned, "I guess any one of our ideas is as good as another."

"Yeah," Dale said almost inaudibly, trying to validate himself. Nobody said anything for nearly thirty seconds. "What a zoo," Dale whispered to himself.

"Can I get a glass of water?" Antonia asked. Jim nodded and walked to the adjoining kitchen, returning with a glass. Phoebe was thirsty, too, but didn't want to ask anyone for anything. She'd just added all five of them to her list of people she hated.

Chuck finally stood. "Well," he started with an oddly casual tone, "I think I'd better get home to my wife." Eyes widened with surprise. Phoebe laughed.

"You've got to be kidding," Phoebe said, "you can't go home to your wife now, she won't even recognize you."

"I know that," Chuck said, "but we don't have a plan and she's probably wondering what happened to me. I don't want her to worry."

"Oh, she'll be worried," Phoebe said. Antonia shook her head slowly. Was she shaking it because of Chuck, Phoebe, or the situation in general?

Jim tried to make Chuck understand: "Chuck, listen—" It was just then that he heard a truck and trailer pulling up his unpaved driveway. He stepped quickly to the window, peering out. "Shoot!" he exclaimed, "It's Eric."

"Who's Eric?" Axl asked.

"Eric Lopez," Jim said. "He owns a farm outside of Minersville. You met him once a couple summers ago. I forgot he was coming to sell me a horse today."

Axl remembered Dale's performance at Hometown Inn. "Should I tell him to leave?" Axl asked, rising to his feet. He still hadn't gotten used to being so tall.

Jim furrowed his boyish brow again. "No," he said, "Eric's moving out of town soon so I don't know that he'll come back." He thought hard and quickly, but judiciously. Finally, he took off his cowboy hat and set it aside. "Okay, listen, Axl. We'll go out there together. Be me but don't overdo it. I'll look at the horse and make little observations. Just agree with everything I say. I'll decide whether or not we want it."

The others stayed a conservative distance from the window as they watched the man in the truck step out. He was a little under six feet tall and with black hair streaked with gray. Eric's mother was a first-generation Mexican-American. His father came from an almost uninterrupted line of Shoshone Indians. In appearance Eric was most evidently Native American, with conspicuous cheekbones and an angular jawline, thin eyes, and leathery brown skin. He wore jeans that made his legs look deceptively thin and a matching denim jacket that made his torso look deceptively wide. This Spaghetti Western costume was crowned with a pinched-front cowboy hat fraying at the edges from use. Brodie greeted him familiarly and Eric scratched the dog behind the ears, surveying the scene. He made a step toward the house but halted when Axl and Jim came out the front door.

"Morning, Jim," Eric called, walking casually to the trailer behind his pickup and working on the latch.

Jim winked at Axl deliberately, reminding Axl that *he* was "Jim." "Morning, Eric Lopez," Axl replied awkwardly. He and Jim both winced. He was doing the best "Uncle Jim" impression he could muster, but he was off to a rough start.

"I heard you're moving," Jim cut in as Eric led the horse out of the trailer, "where to?"

Eric tried not to grimace. "I have family down near Fort Hall," he answered, "Sunday morning my wife and the kids and I are all headed down there to stay with them until I get back on my feet." Jim started inspecting the horse. He cast Axl a sideways glance, indicating that he should inspect the horse too. "It's a shame to leave the farm," Eric continued, "it's been in my family for generation after generation."

"What's wrong with it?" Axl asked, trying to think of what Jim would say.

"It's just old and run-down and infertile," Eric admitted frankly. "I'm a terrible farmer and a worse businessman—my dad would've been ashamed, God rest him." He tilted his hat up a little. "Our house is home but I'm afraid it's not worth much either. They're both on the market if you want them."

Jim squinted at the horse after a few slow orbits. The horse looked like it had once been tall and strong and active but was now withering from age and neglect. Its pale white coat had grown coarse and blotched and its ashen mane was tangled. The only apparent remnants of its long career as a trick horse were its large, alert, intelligent-looking black eyes. But these were not enough to redeem its otherwise pitiful condition.

"Eric, you're a good friend," Jim said, "but I gotta tell you: I think I'd sooner buy your house than your horse. Your family has fallen on hard times and this horse sure shows it. Malnourished, sickly, tired. As good of a horseman as I am, I'm just afraid I could never bring him back to full health."

Eric raised a questioning eyebrow. In his fixation on inspecting the horse Jim had forgotten the charade. He hadn't even remembered to drop his distinctive accent. He cast at Axl in panic. Now both of the men were staring at him. "That's exactly right," Axl affirmed awkwardly, "sorry, but he's in pretty rough shape. Don't know that I can buy a horse that looks like that." Eric nodded slowly.

"I'd hoped you wouldn't say that," Eric said, "but I kind of expected it." Without another word he clicked his tongue and led the horse back into the trailer. Axl and Jim waited, controlling their breathing and trying not to make eye contact.

As Eric was closing the trailer he joked, "How serious were you about buying my house?"

Axl chuckled along with him, trying to think of a rationale. "Well...it's like you said: old and run-down and everything."

"Plus it's all the way in Minersville!" Jim added, "But we'll keep our ears open for people looking to buy land up there."

Eric laughed pleasantly. He was clearly disappointed but understood why even a friend as generous as Jim wouldn't buy the horse. It wasn't good for riding and probably wouldn't live much longer, old as it was. Besides, Jim had done business with him before and had been far more generous than the offerings had merited. Eric took a look around him, noting all the telltale signs of construction. "Place looks good," Eric commented before getting back into his truck, "I'll have to come back sometime and see it when it's finished."

"You're always welcome," Axl said, waving. Jim nodded. That's just what he would've said.

When Julie Hocum arrived at the back door of Hometown Inn that day she found Stanley Hobbes unconscious on the ground. The first thing she did was go inside to ask Chuck what had happened. When she found the entire restaurant empty she was confused and a little concerned. Chuck wasn't answering his phone. She finally called Stanley's father to tell him what had happened and then dragged a chair out next to where Stanley lay to wait for Leroy Hobbes to arrive.

Julie was satisfied that Stanley didn't seem badly hurt. He lay in a ragged fetal curl, looking in a lot of ways like a stepped-on spider. His long knobby fingers clutched loosely at his scowling sleeping face which was covered in dirt. Still, there were no apparent signs of anything broken or out of place and he wasn't bleeding so Julie didn't attempt to move him.

She exhaled restfully, leaning back into the shade and resting her hands around her protruding belly as her body relaxed into the chair. She was a very conspicuous six months pregnant. She'd decided that working in a restaurant was the worst occupation for a pregnant woman because the kitchen was always steamy hot and she was always surrounded by delicious food. Chuck had offered to let Julie simply wait tables, but that would mean Chuck would spend less time interacting with the guests. Julie knew that was the part of the job her husband loved best. Besides, she enjoyed cooking and washing in spite of its requiring her being on her feet almost nonstop, which had become quite a workout. Sitting down was an ecstatic sensation every time.

Nevertheless, Julie still preferred to walk to work. She and Chuck lived only ten minutes away by foot and Julie loved being outside when it was warm. She promised herself she'd still go on a walk every day even after she stopped working at the restaurant. Working alongside Chuck in the kitchen was becoming more and more burdensome as her baby grew and Chuck insisted that Julie take a hiatus. Julie always replied, "What would I do at home all day?" Still, she and Chuck knew that it wouldn't be long before she couldn't endure long days of cooking and washing anymore.

Julie was half a head shorter than Chuck (who wasn't all that tall) and much smaller in build, though pregnancy was beginning to make her stouter. She had a lot more freckles than Chuck and her hair was a few shades less red, being more of a strawberry blonde.

While she sat waiting she put her hair back and fit it under Chuck's worn-out baseball cap, which she'd found left on a counter in the kitchen. He'd been wearing it the day they met. Julie had been 22 when she first saw Chuck at a church potluck. He was a few years older than Julie and was different than the boys she'd dated before: boisterous and extroverted, heavyset and a little rough-looking. Yet they'd taken an interest in each other the very first time they met and each had started thinking about marriage almost as soon as they started dating. They had complementary temperaments, corresponding life goals, and a shared love for John Denver and cookie dough. Owning a bed and breakfast in the country had been a dream they'd both had before meeting. Now, after five years of marriage, their dream was materializing.

With it came the fulfillment of another dream: a child. Julie had looked forward for so long to being a mother; she just always thought it would happen before she was twenty-seven. Sometimes dreams come true when you least expect them. And sometimes they're very different from the picture in your head. Julie wondered what her little girl would be like, considering Stanley crumpled up in the dirt. Her daughter might be whole, happy, perhaps even exceptional. But she also might have a lot of challenges. Either way, though, Julie knew that she and Chuck would love their little girl.

Julie could hear Leroy Hobbes' truck coming long before it pulled around behind Hometown Inn. Most trucks in Mackenzie were in dire need of repair: burnt-out headlights, doors held on with bailing twine, smashed windows replaced with wax paper. Leroy's truck was a few accidents away from such a condition, but one tire was a little low and there was a long crack running half the width of the windshield.

Julie smiled welcomingly as the truck pulled to stop, shielding her eyes from the glint of the windshield. She stood up awkwardly as Mr. Hobbes stepped out. They were almost the same height.

"Thanks for the call," Leroy said with a slight suggestion of embarrassment in his voice. His voice was a colorless one; the sort justly ascribed to a man who kept mostly to himself. He stood there looking at Julie for a good ten seconds, his circular eyes unblinking. He made eye contact so infrequently that sometimes it put him in a trance. He reached for the pack of cigarettes in the pocket of his coat and then remembered he was in polite company. He patted himself to conceal the gesture, then unceremoniously bent at the waist and picked his son up, carrying him toward the truck.

Leroy Hobbes was a strong, but small man. Notwithstanding his Carhartt coat, his Levis, and his stubbled face, he seemed out of place on a farm. His features were a collection of bland corporate stereotypes paired with a prevailing air of tired resignation. He had the tense, calculating visage of an accountant with the apologetic downcast stare of a custodian. His farm was quiet and melancholy, much like the man himself. Only he and Stanley lived there, and Stanley usually wasn't there.

Julie didn't know much about Leroy but she could sense that he was upset. He nodded a polite acknowledgment and moved to get back in his truck. "I hope Stanley feels better soon," Julie said with an encouraging smile.

"Yeah, me too." Leroy replied, opening the door.

"He's lucky to have a father who's willing to drop everything and come get him," Julie complimented quickly, trying to squeeze it in before Leroy got in the truck. He paused, still holding the door open. "I hope I can be that kind of parent for my daughter," Julie added, resting a hand on her belly.

Leroy pursed his lips, considering the statement. He still faced the truck's interior. Its worn upholstery was sun-faded, stained, and covered in animal hair. Leroy and Stanley's extinguished cigarettes occupied every cavity. "Yeah," he finally said, "I hope so too." He made as if to get in the truck, then halted. Leroy cast a glance at the figure of his son still unconscious in the truck. Stanley was a little bit taller than his father and was much thinner, with long, narrow features, like his mother's had been. The emaciated boy bore almost no resemblance to his father other than his round, excited-looking eyes. But even those eyes, one gray and one blue, did not match his father's.

In every way including his face, Stanley was a stranger. "Maybe you could do better," Leroy said. He climbed into the driver's seat, closed the door noisily, and left.

Julie watched him drive away, confounded beyond even offering a "goodbye." His voice was sick with regret and loneliness. Julie knew so little about Leroy Hobbes. His wife had abandoned him and their son when Stanley was still very young. Stanley's challenges had been too much for her to endure. Leroy's words and his bearing expressed plainly the truth he'd learned early on in being a single father: he didn't know how to raise a kid on his own. This much, in so few words, Leroy had confessed.

But there was a great deal more that Leroy never said. He hadn't blamed his wife for leaving. Stanley had been pretty wild and Leroy hadn't been a lot of help. He wasn't much of a husband or a father and he knew it.

A lot of people thought Leroy must have been a pretty good father because Stanley always seemed so happy. *They can think that if they want to*, Leroy had thought to himself after an instance of underserved praise, *but I've got nothing to do with it. Nothing. Not me. Somebody helped him get through school, somebody puts him in a good mood. Heck, the kid hasn't asked me for cigarettes in weeks, somebody besides me helped him quit smoking. I don't know who. Teachers from school, friends from town, God? And I'm no Christian, but I figure when a kid who has a father like me and problems like Stanley can still be happy, then there's got to be more to life than what life gives you.*

In truth, Leroy barely knew his son. Stanley was his own man and always had been. Leroy was too busy on the farm to spend much time with his son and Stanley was too clumsy to help out much. When

Leroy wasn't working, Stanley had usually wandered off somewhere—and Leroy never minded because he was always tired.

Sometimes they'd watch TV together but that's about as close as they ever got to the family Leroy had always hoped for. The Norman Rockwell kind of family: lots of kids, Mom and Dad sitting next to each other at the head of the table, smiling faces. Leroy wanted to teach his boys to play football. Stanley didn't even like football. No, Leroy didn't really know what his boy liked. Or where he spent all of his time. In fact, if Leroy didn't hear him snoring occasionally or pass by him having a snack in the kitchen at night, he'd think he lived alone.

Most unsettling of all was this: Leroy would dream that he was Stanley sometimes. All of a sudden he'd just be lying in Stanley's bed alone in the night. Dreams like that took days to recover from. It was just so lonely and dark in his son's room; scary, even. It could only make Leroy wonder why Stanley preferred being in his room or wandering around town so much more than spending any time around his father.

For the first time in a long time, Julie realized that not everyone in the world was looking forward to something. It was a distressing thought, one that made her heart ache for the little man. She said a quiet prayer for Leroy Hobbes.

CHAPTER NINE

THE BARBER

After another grueling session of argument, the others finally decided to give Chuck one hour to go and explain everything to his wife, but not before setting some ground rules:

First, any decision made by the group had to be made unanimously. This was everyone's problem and it was likely they'd need all of them in order to fix it.

Second, Atlas Ranch would be their home until they figured out what to do. Jim got everyone to agree to this only with the concession that during the day they could leave to try any reversal experiment they thought might be effective. They planned on returning to Hometown Inn that evening as well as the next day.

Third, wherever anybody went they had to take their counterpart with them. This went almost without saying, but Dale wanted to make sure that Chuck didn't run off with his body. Dale's body wasn't much but Dale couldn't recall experiencing anything quite as uncomfortable as Chuck's husky, hairy body.

Fourth and last, they were to show respect for the bodies they now inhabited and always defer to the rightful owner for any major decisions. This had been Antonia's idea. Her body was the product of years and years of dedicated training. It was an insured investment for several wealthy sponsors and was a point of pride for legions of fans around the globe.

It was convenient that their souls had been traded between pairs rather than in random sequence but Antonia still wished her body had gone to somebody besides Phoebe. Jim, maybe—he seemed responsible. He was the natural choice for the "leader" of the group: under pressure he'd assumed the role of mediator and had executed his duties well; he'd been hospitable to total strangers; and he was doing much better at remembering who everybody was than the others.

Dale was having the greatest difficulty. He'd finally become so frustrated that he asked Chuck for the paper and pencil stub that were in his back pocket. With them he wrote a chart:

Brain	*Body*
Axil	*Jim*
Jim	*Axil*
Antonia	*Jess*
Jess	*Antonia*
Me	*Chuck*

| *Chuck* | *Me* |

"I think Axl is just 'A-X-L,'" Chuck offered as Dale reviewed the chart. They'd just gotten back in Jim's truck. Jim was letting Chuck borrow it to drive back to his house.

"Thanks," Dale murmured, a little embarrassed. He pulled the pencil stub out of his pocket again and made the correction, then buckled his seatbelt. Dale wasn't a scholarly or creative man. He hadn't even been able to think of a pseudonym when the situation called for it: Dale Merchant was, indeed, his real name.

Dale was a barber. He drove an inexpensive car and still lived in the modest home he'd grown up in. His life, he believed, was one of little consequence. He wasn't totally dissatisfied with it, but he also felt that there were few things to take great pride in. He minded his own business and maintained a comfortable, predictable life. He was simple—not stupid, as some people thought—just simple.

His performance in school had been mediocre and his performance in the workplace was just above average. He worked in a barbershop in a nearby town that was several times larger than Mackenzie but was equally obscure. He had little money but managed it prudently, never having developed expensive or excessive tastes. He'd never travelled much, and nowadays he only left Mackenzie every once in a great while. Dale's singular defining characteristic was his resemblance to the actor Don Knotts, a likeness he was inevitably reminded of at least once a week. True, his eyes were a little buggier and his ears were a little bigger but the semblance was close enough to justify frequent requests for pictures. He'd once even been requested for a birthday party.

Dale's life was one that was full of goals that were written down and never revisited. He always kept a folded-up piece of paper in his rear trouser pocket with a companion stub of a pencil. Every few days he'd take them out and write down a goal—usually one that his employer or his mother (who he'd lived with until her death earlier that year) had compelled him to make. Dale liked the novelty of goals and the prospect of change, but routine always won in the end. The man was effortlessly consistent in his habits.

Dale did sometimes imagine a more distinguished, more eventful life, but to say that Dale's imagination was unambitious would be an understatement. Buying a pair of expensive shoes and receiving a few unsolicited compliments would have fulfilled all the fantasies that Dale had in a week. This recent turn of events could mean a whole lifetime of changes but Dale had a bad feeling about the near future.

It was a quiet drive to Chuck's house. Dale was a decent conversationalist on his best days, but today he was literally not himself. Chuck, true to form, had tried to start conversations with Dale but had failed. As a barber Dale understood that small talk and gossip were part of his job and when he did them on his own terms in familiar places like the barber shop he was pretty good at them. But outside of brief encounters with customers Dale was cautious when meeting new people and his favored brand of caution was suspicious paranoia. He'd never even shared his name with Chuck on any of the occasions he'd eaten at Hometown Inn.

"Pretty wild stuff today, huh?" Chuck said.

"Yep," Dale replied.

"How are you holding out?"

"I think I'm fine."

Chuck went to scratch his beard. He didn't have one. He became conscious of Dale's body again. "Nice of you to lend yourself to me for a while," Chuck grinned.

Dale seemed surprised. "How can you make jokes at a time like this?"

"Sorry," Chuck apologized pleasantly, "I just figured I'd make the best of it."

"Well there is no 'best', Pollyanna," Dale said. "You're trapped in my body and I'm trapped in your body and there isn't a person alive who knows what to do about it. It's a zoo, that's what it is—an absolute zoo!"

Chuck paused to wait for the tension to wear off, then proceeded with caution. "Well at least you can take the day off work," he smiled. Dale didn't respond. "What is it you do for work, Dale?"

"I'm a barber," he said mechanically, then clammed up, realizing he'd revealed personal information.

"You've got me beat there," Chuck said. "If I tried to cut someone's hair I'd probably give them a lobotomy." A single edge of Dale's mouth curled with a smile. Chuck put a hand on top of the steering wheel. "This is a nice watch," Chuck complimented. "Where'd you get it?" It wasn't really that great of a watch; Chuck was just trying to be his friendly, conversational self.

"My mother gave it to me for my birthday three years ago," Dale answered, "I never was big on watches, but Mom never was good at giving gifts either."

Chuck gave a satisfied chuckle. "Well, it's the thought that counts. Your mom is still around then?"

Dale wasn't sure how to interpret the question. "I'm younger than I look, you know," he said.

Chuck realized his pretenses were failing. His questions were becoming less and less meaningful; he was just trying to keep the conversation going. "Yes, I'm sure you are. I didn't mean that the way it sounded. Your mom lives around here, then?"

Dale was more careful this time. "You know, I think I've said enough about myself for today."

The tension was back. "That's fine," Chuck said accommodatingly. "That's just fine." Chuck was silent for a while. "Has anybody ever told you that you look like Barney Fife?"

"Yeah," Dale sighed, "I get that a lot."

Dale had been staring out the window all this time. Eye contact wasn't one of his strong suits. He didn't need it much as a barber. Besides, there wasn't much to see: the ranch was a few miles south of town partway down a long dirt road that one could drive on all day and never find anything but trees and rocks and hills. There are a lot of roads like that in Idaho. Dale wondered for the first time why people built roads that led to nowhere. What was the goal? End the road in some remote pocket in the mountains and hope someone would build a town there, that people would flock to it simply because there was a road that led to it? He could believe that's how Minersville came to be. But maybe it was opposite—maybe the hope was that, if they carried on long enough, eventually they'd find something worth building a road to. But what could they have found here?

As they came back into town they passed by Dale's home, a modest doublewide trailer where he'd lived his whole thirty-nine years of life. He wasn't ashamed of living in a trailer; most of the people he knew lived in trailers. In fact, he had many fond memories of growing up there, but now that his mother wasn't there it didn't seem like much of a home anymore. Her passing had been tough: she'd been his best and most constant friend. He grimaced weakly as they passed by: it looked so hollow. Coming home from work every day had become less and less enticing month to month, a disappointment akin to opening a refrigerator and finding nothing but a can of stale corn that had been opened up and forgotten. It stood in stark, dismal contrast to his simple, pleasant childhood. It was an atmosphere so uninviting that it almost made his present circumstances seem not so bad. As scary as the morning had been, this had been the most variety, excitement, and companionship that Dale had had in a very long time. For a moment he wondered if he really wanted his old life back.

Chuck lived on the other end of town (which here means a five-minute drive) near the restaurant. It was a little blue house not much bigger than some of the doublewides in town. Its lawn was patchy and its sidewalk was uneven, but it was home. Underneath the awning where the Hocums parked their car they found a little bit of space for "outside" toys for the baby: things they'd bought knowing she wouldn't be able to play with them for years. The letters on the welcome mat were nearly worn off from use by visitors. Outwardly it was not much grander than Dale's own home but it had an unmistakably welcoming air about it. It was more than a house: it was a home.

Chuck, of course, walked ahead and opened the front door without a thought of his unfamiliar appearance. Julie was sitting on the couch talking to her mother on the phone when the strange man entered unannounced. Everybody wonders what they'd say to an intruder. Julie said, "Just a sec, Mom," into the phone, turned to the man and asked, "Can I help you?"

"Jules, it's me," Chuck said with a smile, relieved to see his wife in good spirits. Dale walked in behind him.

"Hi, love," she said to the man who appeared to be her husband, "What happened? Why'd you close the restaurant? And who's your friend?"

Dale gave a weak "uh…," casting back and forth from Chuck to Julie. He cleared his throat, scratched his neck, then stood in dumbfounded silence.

Chuck closed the door, taking a discreet glance outside to make sure nobody was within earshot. He seated himself on the armchair neighboring Julie's couch. Julie flinched a little bit, clearly uneasy at the stranger's approach. "Jules, listen," he told her earnestly, "there was a terrible accident at the inn this morning. We don't know all the details and aren't really sure what our next step is, but I really need you to believe me on this."

"Believe what? What happened?" Julie asked, a little frustration in her voice over the roundabout answers and her husband's apparent silence. "And who are you?"

Chuck widened his buggy eyes and spoke slowly for emphasis. "I'm Charles Robert Hocum, your husband."

Immediately Julie's brow furrowed. She shifted her gaze back to the man who looked like her husband. Dale nodded his head and muttered a concurrence: "Oh, yeah."

"Chuck," Julie implored to Dale, "what's he talking about? What's this all about?"

The true Chuck answered once more. "I don't know, babe, that's what I'm telling you. Today at the inn there was some sort of crazy...I don't know...some sort of phenomenon. Some weird sort of science fiction thing. Geez, I know this is going to be hard to believe! All our brains switched bodies, Jules, we don't know how. We're still trying to figure out what to do about it."

Julie was silent throughout Chuck's frantic testimony. She nodded subtly, a million possible scenarios running through her head as to why her husband might be playing along with this hoax, each one as unlikely as the next. She swallowed the lump in her throat, determined to command the situation. This man was obviously using some sort of leverage against Chuck, otherwise he'd never have gone along with it. "I want you to leave," she told the man, his cartoonish face showing the sting of rejection. "Go out the back door and wait in the far corner of the backyard where you can't hear us. I want to speak to my husband alone."

"Jules—" Chuck started. He then decided that he was willing to do whatever it took for his wife to believe him. He nodded compliantly, mouthed an "ok," and then passed Dale on his way to the kitchen, making deliberate eye contact with him. He opened the back door and offered his wife a final "I love you" as he left.

Julie waited several seconds before she stood up, walked over to near where Dale stood so she could have a clear view of the back yard and the strange man through the kitchen window. When he was at the far corner she turned to the man she believed to be her husband and spoke at library volume.

"Who is that guy?" she asked.

Dale breathed a few nervous breaths and licked his lips as if priming them for explanation. His voice tremulous at first, he answered, "He's, well...uh....he's...telling the truth. He is your husband, honest! He's Chuck, not me. The whole thing is crazy—a zoo, that's what it is—but he's right, I'm not Chuck, he is."

"Then who are you?" Julie asked accusingly, becoming increasingly frustrated at everyone's dedication to this façade. Dale's scatterbrained manner was making her anxious on top of everything.

"I-I-I'm Dale Merchant," he admitted, forgetting his paranoid anonymity, "we only just met today, honest. I was just minding my own breakfast, eating business, then wham-o, here we are! Honest, it's-it's...it's a zoo, that's all..."

Julie's head was angry but her heart was sad. She'd never seen Chuck act anything like this and the man's manner alone was almost enough to convince her. Even with Chuck's voice, his unique accent and inflections made him sound like he was doing an impression of somebody else.

Julie walked into the kitchen, opened the back door, and called, "Come back in!" As she walked back to the living room she stared at the ground breathing shallowly. The two men stood obediently by the door while Julie, with some difficulty in maneuvering her pregnant body, sat back down.

"I want to talk to him alone," she said to the man who appeared to be Chuck, dismissing him. He said nothing; he just went—with some relief—out of house into the back yard. He was back within seconds, even before a word had been spoken. "Sorry," he stammered with some embarrassment through a forced smile, "didn't realize you had a dog back there. I've got this thing about dogs is all." He said all this almost without stopping and excused himself out the front door instead.

When she was sure they were truly alone, Julie gathered her wits and again asked, "Okay, who are you?"

"I swear to you, Jules, it's me: I'm Chuck."

"Convince me," she said with the same tone as a mother whose child swore they hadn't broken a vase.

"Well, my name is Charles Robert Hocum, born May 29th—"

"Not birthdays," Julie interrupted, "there's no way I'm going to believe your story unless you can tell me something that only Chuck would know."

Chuck thought hard for a long while, keeping eye contact while he considered the question. "We watched *The Sound of Music* last night—" he began to say.

"It was on TV," Julie interrupted, "there are a million ways you might have known that."

"—and you couldn't get over how much you wished they made movies like that nowadays," Chuck finished.

"A lot of people think that," she defended, secretly a little closer to buying his story. Still, it wasn't enough for her to go off of.

"You've never had the chicken pox," Chuck offered. Julie shook her head.

"Still not convinced."

Chuck thought harder, imploring Julie with his eyes.

"I wet the bed on our wedding night," he finally said. She was silent for a long time, trying to come up with a way that someone would know that.

"Room service would have known," she suggested, "they changed our sheets—"

"We washed the sheets ourselves, remember?" he interrupted. Julie clammed up with a look of stubborn skepticism that was slowly giving way to tears.

"Well, I don't—" she began with a quivering lip.

"Jules," Chuck interrupted again, stepping forward and taking her wrist in his familiar way, "it's me. I don't know how this happened, but you've got to believe me. I'm your husband."

Tears rolled down Julie's cheeks. She swallowed hard a few times, cleared her throat, and whispered, "I know." She didn't want it to be true. It was terrible and scary, but she knew her husband would never go along with a prank like this. Chuck wasn't sure what to say next. He was glad that his wife trusted him, but there was little comfort for her. She spoke next, wiping the tears from her cheeks and sniffling. "So, what are we going to do now?"

"I don't know," Chuck admitted, heaving a sigh that, against his nature, was not at all optimistic. "There are four others besides me and Dale—the same thing happened to them. They're all at Jim Boyd's ranch south of town. We're all going to go back to the Inn tonight to see if it'll happen again."

"What exactly happened?" Julie implored.

Chuck was slow to answer. "I don't know how to explain it. I was just in the kitchen working and all of a sudden there was some sort of...commotion. I felt like someone was picking me up by the head and tossing me into the dining room—but not my whole body, just my soul. Jules, I don't think I've ever felt my soul before, but I did then."

Julie nodded encouragingly. She didn't actually understand, but she was encouraged that the strange man's speech sounded like her husband's. Chuck's speech was relaxed and flowing while Dale's was tense and higher-pitched. Chuck rehearsed the rest of his day to her, not leaving anything out so as to lend maximum credibility to his claim of being Chuck. As he talked Julie collected herself, and by the time Chuck finished his account she was herself again.

"Well I guess I've learned my lesson," she said after Chuck stopped talking. "I let you run the restaurant by yourself for one morning and *this* happens!" She laughed. Chuck laughed too, glad to have his wife back. Dale, who waited outside and could hear the laughter, would never ask its cause, but he'd always wonder how the interview could possibly have started with anger and suspicion and ended with laughter.

CHAPTER TEN
THE FIGHTER

Antonia and Phoebe were in Antonia's Porsche again. It looked so natural and glamorous for the beautiful black celebrity to be sitting at the helm of the flashy white sports car, but to have the scrawny nondescript teenager driving it was almost comical—especially with the fighter sitting in the passenger's seat.

"What is this we're listening to?" Phoebe asked.

"Beastie Boys," Antonia answered.

"Do all of their songs suck this bad?"

"Are you for real?" Antonia fumed in exasperation, "What's your problem? Stop criticizing my music!"

"I wouldn't have to if you listened to real music." Phoebe smirked.

"Yeah, like what?" Antonia demanded. Phoebe pretended she didn't hear. She didn't want her own tastes demeaned.

It was nearly three o'clock in the afternoon when the group finally returned to Hometown Inn. Julie Hocum decided the best thing she could do to help was to join the company of strangers and cook a meal for them. Given the hour, nobody was quite sure whether it was lunch or dinner. Chuck, of course, insisted on helping her prepare the meal, as did Antonia. Antonia said that it would help to take her mind off of the situation. In truth, Antonia just needed some time away from Phoebe. Phoebe had been harassing her all day and she'd nearly exhausted Antonia's reserves of "cool." Besides, Antonia was a decent cook—she'd even competed on a celebrity episode of *Chopped*. She hadn't won, but she also hadn't been the first one eliminated.

The kitchen had to be cleaned first, crusty and oily pans and silverware having been abandoned for hours. Chuck's one-man show that morning had left the kitchen in complete disarray; he hadn't even thought to put his ingredients away when they left for the ranch. Still, Antonia appreciated the chance to help out and needed the normalcy of menial chores.

As one can imagine, Chuck and Julie didn't open the restaurant back up that day, at least not while the strangers were there. If the paranormal event reoccurred, they didn't want to chance any interference. With the Hocums and Antonia in the kitchen, everyone else sat at a table in the dining area talking—all except for Phoebe, who defiantly sat at a nearby table from which she could listen in while appearing to keep herself aloof.

Since the time that Chuck and Dale had left to talk to Julie, the others had had a brief tour of Atlas Ranch and then spent quite a bit of time on the internet researching their problem. "Did you turn anything up?" Dale asked once they were seated.

"Not a lot," Axl answered. "Believe it or not, WebMD doesn't have a ton of entries on soul transference."

Jim sighed. "You know you're in a bad way when the most helpful websites for your situation are about science fiction and witchcraft," he said.

"They were helpful, though?" Dale asked hopefully.

"A little bit," Jim answered with a grimace. "One thing I read says it's called *corporeal transference*. Can you imagine any other time I would've had to learn that? Now all we need is some sort of psychic or druid or something to change us back." Jim smiled but nobody laughed. "There's also something called *astral projection*, but I guess that's just your soul leaving its body, not necessarily finding a new one. Honestly, Dale, right now I'm leaning more toward hypnotism or insanity."

"Insanity for sure," Phoebe commented. The others cast fleeting glances at her. Dale kept staring.

"What are you looking at?" Phoebe demanded accusingly, "Haven't you ever seen a black person before?"

"Well no, not in person," Dale replied sheepishly.

Phoebe was about to roll her eyes when she noticed the earnestness in Dale's expression. "You're kidding me," she said, betraying some shock, "you've never seen an African American in real life?"

Dale diverted his gaze and sunk in his chair a little, muttering, "Well, it's Idaho, you know…"

Antonia came out around then and handed each of them a menu. She smiled and said in an exaggerated drawl, "Hey there, welcome to Hometown Inn! I couldn't help but notice you boys have your brains switched up. Luckily for you we're running a corporeal transference special right now—order whatever you want on the house!" Jim and Axl laughed, grateful for the levity. It took Dale a moment to realize she was joking, but he laughed too. At first he'd thought her soul had been switched again.

The only one who didn't laugh was Phoebe who, upon receiving her menu, said in her sarcastic way, "Big day, huh? First time working a real job?" Antonia had a hundred venomous words boiling at the back of her throat but swallowed them, held her breath, smiled, and then cast her eyes to the ceiling as she walked away. Normally she *liked* being civil.

The others had heard the comment and didn't seem to know how to start talking again. Jim, of course, finally did. "Jess, right?" Jim asked her.

It took Phoebe a moment to realize he was talking to her. She hadn't been named "Jess" for very long. "Yeah, why?" she said defensively.

"It's a good name," Jim answered. "My wife's name was Jess."

"Thanks," she replied flatly. She wished people would stop being friendly to her, it was really annoying.

"Where are you from, Jess?" Jim asked.

"Washington," she lied.

"Where in Washington?" Axl chimed in. "I'm from the Seattle area."

"Spokane," she lied again. She had no idea where Spokane was, but she seemed to remember it being a city in Washington.

"Huh" was all Axl said in reply. Phoebe wondered if they knew she was lying.

"So what's your story?" Jim said, continuing his interview.

"My story?" she returned, the tone of her voice warning that she was already preparing a sarcastic response. "My story is that I've had about enough of everybody I run into sticking their noses into my business—that's my story." Dale and Axl drew quick breaths that they held. Jim raised his eyebrows. "Look," Phoebe continued, slightly more diplomatically, "I appreciate you helping me and everybody out, but trust me, we don't wanna be friends. So let's figure out how to fix this and let's all get on with our lives, huh?"

"Fair enough," Jim said respectfully.

Antonia, who'd heard the conversation from the other side of the kitchen door, poked her head in and said with an apologetic smile, "Just for the record, she's not me, ok? Remember that once we're ourselves again."

"Yeah, don't get us mixed up," Phoebe sneered, arresting Antonia's attention, "Toni over here has a reputation to uphold. What would the world do if they found out she wasn't the easygoing sunbeam she seems to be in the ring?"

"It's Antonia, not Toni," came the fighter's frustrated reply, "don't make me tell you again."

"What are you gonna do to me?" Phoebe shot back tauntingly.

Antonia stepped out of the kitchen and squared up with her. Antonia couldn't remember ever getting so hostile outside of the ring, at least not in a long time. "I'm Antonia LeBlanc," she said, "I'll do whatever I want."

"Barely," Phoebe smirked, "I've got four inches and thirty pounds on you, blondie. As far as I'm concerned, *I'm* Antonia LeBlanc."

"Fine," Antonia said. In one swift motion Antonia grabbed Phoebe's wrist with one hand and her elbow with the other, contorting them painfully and wrenching Phoebe's arm behind her back. Phoebe shrieked and crashed chest-down on the table, then grunted angrily as she struggled with her face pressed against it. Antonia was surprised how difficult it was to maneuver her opponent now that she was in the smaller body. Still, her technique lacked nothing.

Jim, Dale, and Axl jumped up from their seats, ready to intercede. The Hocums poked their heads in from the kitchen. "You know what you don't have?" Antonia continued, "Sixteen years of training, that's what." Phoebe continued to struggle and grunt, strained curses squeezing out like air from a tire.

"Antonia, I don't think that's helping," Jim implored.

Antonia was having a lot of difficulty restraining her powerful former self even with all her weight leaned on top of her. She was all but straddling Phoebe as she brought her mouth down next to Phoebe's ear. "Who's Antonia LeBlanc?" Antonia demanded.

"Me," Phoebe wheezed. She shrieked weakly as Antonia twisted her arm harder.

"Not good!" Axl said.

"Don't hurt her, Antonia," Jim said, taking a couple steps toward them, not sure if he should intercede.

"Sorry, who?" Antonia growled into Phoebe's ear, as if not hearing the others.

Phoebe flared her nose. "You're only...hurting...yourself," Phoebe grunted haltingly, "I don't care...break it." At this realization Antonia finally released Phoebe and took a few steps back, panting. Her new body was already weary. Phoebe got to her feet, rubbing the joints and inflamed skin of the affected arm and glaring at Antonia. She hissed something profane under her breath.

The others let out sighs of relief, including Chuck and Julie, who now stood just outside the kitchen door. Dale muttered something about a zoo. Antonia looked around into their frightened and uncomfortable faces. "Sorry," she offered sincerely to the group, tucking the bangs of her blonde hair behind her ears.

Jim put a boyish hand on her shoulder. "You ok?" he asked.

She waited a long time to answer, then simply said "yeah." Jim turned to Phoebe, "How about you, Jess?" She didn't answer. She just shook her head, trying in vain to hold back the tears that slowly streamed from her dark angry face. She glowed with the heat of embarrassment—hot ears, hot cheeks, hot eyes. Phoebe ran into the bathroom to hide, slamming the door and locking it. Jim sighed and ran his hand through his hair.

Antonia washed dishes in silence. Few things dealt a greater blow to her confidence than losing her temper. Self-control had been the most difficult skill to acquire in her career, a skill that she considered a distinguishing mark of class and maturity for a fighter. Antonia had learned to respond to petty insults and opposition like an adult. Episodes like this made her feel like a kid again.

However wealthy or accomplished Antonia became, she hoped people would also think of her as sophisticated, clever, and level-headed; this was the image she'd worked so hard to create. As much as she loved her sport, she hated the associated stereotypes. She was a professional: she dressed like a professional, she trained like a professional, she spoke like a professional, and she conducted herself like a professional. Antonia viewed herself as a refined, talented athlete, not just some brute brawler. But losing her temper made Antonia feel like she was giving herself too much credit.

Antonia was usually slow to anger and usually took criticism with grace. She was extremely vain, it was true, which made both habits difficult to maintain. They had come to her through no small amount of practice. Still, she had a threshold, and Phoebe seemed to have a natural knack for getting under Antonia's skin.

After several minutes of washing dishes and piling them up on the counter, Antonia became aware of Julie next to her, towel-drying the dishes. Antonia cast a sideways glance at her, still not totally withdrawn from her self-engrossment. Julie smiled reassuringly, keeping her eyes on her work to avoid provoking Antonia.

"I wouldn't worry about it," Julie comforted. "Everyone's had a really hard day—they all understand."

Antonia heaved a big sigh. "*I* don't understand," she said, "*I* don't get it." She and Julie resumed their tasks.

The silence was maddening. Chuck called out from the walk-in freezer: "Hey, Jules, wanna turn on the radio?" She turned it on.

Chuck reentered carrying assorted meats. "Who's this we're listening to?" he asked.

Julie was about to say that she didn't know when Antonia answered, "Whitney Houston."

"Oh, do you like this song?" Julie asked, turning up the volume a little.

"I like all her songs." Antonia smiled a little. "Besides, I'm from New Jersey. I *have* to like Whitney Houston."

"Where are you from in Jersey?" Chuck asked, and then added with a comic tone, "As if I know anything about New Jersey…"

"Medford," Antonia answered.

"You grew up there, then?" Julie asked.

"Yeah," Antonia said, "well, kind of. We lived in Medford but my dad worked in Philadelphia so my siblings and I went to a charter school there."

"And where did you learn martial arts?" Julie asked.

"In Philly," Antonia said. "There are a lot of studios in Philly and my dad had one near his work. I'd go there after school a few nights a week."

"That sounds fun," Julie smiled, "How old were you when you started?"

"I was ten."

"That young?" Chuck exclaimed, "Really? What made you want to get into it?"

"A bunch of kids at school did it and told me I should check it out."

This was so typical of Antonia LeBlanc: get involved in something simply to be social and then become the best. She would always accept the invitation, always take the dare, always up the ante. Whatever the circumstances that put her in a situation, Antonia invariably viewed it as a competition, and she took competition seriously. Because of this she'd achieved praiseworthy prowess in a number of skills. She started playing the guitar when she was six and began taking vocal lessons shortly thereafter. She displayed natural talent in school theater productions both in singing and in acting. Scholastically she maintained good grades notwithstanding her several involvements. In each of these she showed enthusiasm and excellence, but her true investiture was in the praise of others. Yes, Antonia LeBlanc was excellent because she loved being appreciated and paid attention to. In Antonia's life, being admired was the most alluring reward of all.

Whether or not Antonia realized it, this was the reason that Phoebe was so skilled at upsetting her. Antonia's enemies in the UFC were often disrespectful but she always made them eat their words in the ring. But at the peril of harming herself, Antonia now realized she couldn't do that to Phoebe. It was an awful irony: a vile seventeen-year-old who hadn't even learned to have proper respect for her own body now had control of Antonia's masterpiece and the elaborate persona that went with it. If she had a mind to, Phoebe could trash Antonia's good name beyond repair, make her seem like a fake—not to mention her potential for ruining Antonia's very carefully constructed body. It wasn't fair, Antonia thought, that this ragged brat should be given stewardship over her, even for a day. That's when Antonia received a very important stroke of inspiration.

"Pause," she said, taking a waitress's notebook, "I'm gonna go see what everyone wants for dinner." Exiting the kitchen, she asked a brief and general "Has everybody decided yet?", but not waiting for a response she continued straight to the ladies' bathroom, knocking on the door.

"Whoever it is, I'm not interested," came Phoebe's reply from behind the locked door.

"Jess, I'm so, so sorry," Antonia said in all sincerity.

"You know, I'll *bet* you are," came the unconvincing reply.

"I really, really am. I never should have exploded at you like that and I definitely never should have touched you. We've all had a really bad day and you deserve just as much patience as anyone."

Phoebe was silent for a moment. "Sure," she said. "Thank you. Now go away."

Antonia's voice was quieter. "I can make it up to you."

"Listen, Toni, I don't want your sympathy, ok? I don't want to make up with you to save face, I don't want to be your friend, and I definitely don't want—"

"I want to hire you," Antonia cut her off. Phoebe made her wait a long time for a response. She relished the tension she was putting Antonia through. Finally, Antonia heard the door unlock.

"Come into my office," Phoebe said. Antonia entered and closed the door behind her. She'd never conducted business in such a crude setting before—it was humiliating, but she figured that that was Phoebe's intention so she pretended not to be affected. Phoebe sat on the closed toilet, seeming as attentive and comfortable as if it had been her own bedroom. In the corner there was a stainless steel trash can with a flat lid. Antonia pulled it up and sat on it.

"You're a runaway, aren't you?" Antonia asked point-blank. Phoebe was obviously caught off guard by the question, but didn't want to seem vulnerable.

"Yes I am," she said with conviction, concealing the shame that had been creeping into her conscience throughout that day.

"I could tell," Antonia said. "How long have you been on your own?"

"About six months," Phoebe lied.

Antonia stared at her skeptically, but not wishing to irritate the girl further she said, "Well, I don't want to lecture you and it's none of my business. I'm sure you had your reasons, but whatever they were you seem pretty desperate now. You're probably pretty low on money, huh?"

"Maybe," Phoebe answered cautiously. "Let's cut to you hiring me. What did you have in mind?"

Antonia stared more earnestly. "You should know that my reputation is extremely important to me. When people recognize me and want to talk to me or ask for my autograph they always expect me to be friendly and classy and I want to keep it that way. I'm always civil, even to the people I beat up—"

"What does that have to do with—" Phoebe cut her off.

"Just listen!" Antonia said, arresting the conversation once more. "It's also extremely important how I treat my body."

"Yeah, I can tell," Phoebe mocked, rubbing her aching wrist.

"Sorry," Antonia said dismissively, "but as I was saying, it's been a ton of work getting into the shape I'm in and maintaining it. What's more it's essential to my career. I don't know how long we're going to have to endure this awful situation, but if it's going to be more than just today I need to know that I'm going to get my old body back."

"So you want to hire me to exercise?" Phoebe asked, intrigued.

"Not just that," Antonia clarified. "I want you to be me in public. Any time we're not at Atlas Ranch I want you to be all smiles and hugs, just like me. Any time we're at Atlas Ranch I want you to exercise and eat exactly the way I tell you."

"I haven't exercised a day in my life!" Phoebe laughed. It wasn't totally true, but nearly.

"But I have!" Antonia responded. "Your new body is a masterpiece—you're welcome. But that's my deal. You will eat what I tell you to, you will act how I tell you to. No sarcasm. No tantrums. And if you keep your end of the deal I'll pay you $500 a day."

As destitute as Phoebe was, $500 sounded like a fortune. Still, she was certain Antonia could afford more and she loved pushing her buttons. "Peanuts!" Phoebe mocked. "You underestimate how hard it is for me to be nice. Double that and I'll think about it."

Antonia released a tense sigh. "I hope you know that the way you act is abominable."

"Yeah, I know."

"Fine. $1000 a day, but I reserve the right to cut that in half any time you screw up. And I'm talking, like, if you so much as eat a Twinkie you're only getting $500."

Phoebe put forth her strong black hand. "Deal. What do I get to eat for dinner?"

"We'll get to dinner," Antonia said, clasping the hand, "but first I need you to call a stressed-out film director and an even more stressed-out agent."

Dinner was a great chance for everyone to forget the situation. Talking was a constant reminder of the strange new bodies, but eating and enjoying food was just distracting enough to create the illusion of normalcy. Between the three of them, the Hocums and Antonia had cooked and served the meal in good time, and then out of courtesy everyone helped clean up, even Phoebe. The prospect of making $1000 a day had taken instant effect.

There was a short controversy over whether or not the restaurant should open the next day. Chuck insisted that they could afford to keep it closed for a day or two more even though he knew they couldn't. Julie was sure that she and one or two of their regular staff could easily handle running the restaurant without him, even for partial days if necessary. When she suggested that the present group return for breakfast the next morning, she won the contest by popular vote.

Julie's subsequent calls to her employees brought to many minds a dilemma that Antonia had already faced: contacting those they were accountable to. Jim had sent his workers home for the day, but what about tomorrow? Axl's parents video-called him every evening before bed without fail. Dale, of course, would have to contact his employer if he planned on taking a day off, but he was still convinced that the problem could be slept off like the flu. Chuck did finally talk Dale into letting him make the call, at which point Dale was forced to admit that his name was, in fact, "Dale." He also had to admit that Chuck's impression of him was very good, albeit not very flattering; Chuck was an unrepentant ham and had the others stifling laughter all throughout the phone call.

Phoebe's background and identity were frequent elephants in the room but nobody said anything. Antonia, of course, had already confirmed for herself that Phoebe was a runaway and the others had their suspicions. But "Jess" continued to enjoy anonymity won through deception—save only in the case of Antonia, who secretly had already been through Phoebe's backpack and knew a great deal more about Phoebe than she had revealed. It was a sparse collection: snack food wrappers, a pocket knife, sunglasses, a toothbrush—things like that. The only items useful for Antonia's purposes were Phoebe's wallet and her journal, of which nearly all the pages had been torn out predating her running away.

Had the earlier entries been included, Antonia might have been fairer in her judgements of the girl. Phoebe had become uncharacteristically nasty as of late. True, she'd always been prone to sarcasm and true, she was often being reprimanded by parents and teachers. But Phoebe was altogether a very normal teenager. She liked movies and music and hanging out with friends, she was passionate about her opinions, she had a small collection of insecurities, and she was incessantly doodling on everything, including her hands. Before running away her journal had been equal parts venting about things in her life, celebrating things in her life, and recording secrets about boys she liked. Occasionally she even wrote flattering things about her parents. Tearing out the old pages was part of Phoebe's revenge.

The company of strangers got to know each other better over the next two hours as they waited in vain for another metaphysical upheaval. Jim didn't like the idea that Plan A was simply sitting around doing nothing, but it was all they had. There was no hotline to call, no medication to take—only a very serious problem. Right now keeping everyone calm was his only goal.

Jim, of course, started out making small talk, asking friendly personal questions to get people talking, which they did amidst occasional comic interruptions from Chuck. Inevitably, these interruptions led to Chuck's stand-up comedy routine. Jim had heard the jokes a hundred times before but thought them ideal for taking everybody's minds off the situation. Besides, Chuck's captive audience found him hilarious.

Chuck was his old self again: loud and boisterous, joking and smiling big smiles and telling embarrassing stories to get the others to laugh. Julie was there to contribute, to corroborate, and even to referee her husband's stories when necessary. She'd heard them all so many times that censorship could often be accomplished with no more than a warning look or a hum. Chuck was always careful to respect her wishes—some of the stories were about her.

Jim was in good spirits and made perfect company for Chuck when he was in such a mood. He didn't have the same talent for anecdotes that Chuck had, but his reactions made him an excellent facilitator. He was, of course, also the self-appointed leader and mediator, and felt responsible for making sure everybody felt comfortable, included, and distracted. "Distracted" was an acceptable substitute for "optimistic" at this point.

By close association with his uncle, Axl felt some of the weight of responsibility on his shoulders, too, especially because he now *looked* like his uncle. But for the time he felt safe and carefree, thoroughly enjoying Chuck's antics and anecdotes as he always did. In circles with his peers Axl was an occasional clown, too, so he threw in a funny comment or story once or twice during Chuck's routine. Chuck was always sure to over-indulge the boy with his reaction.

Dale wasn't used to such lively company and was really enjoying himself—not emoting loudly or conspicuously, but clearly feeling genuine levity for once. He contributed nothing other than an eager expression every time there was a lull in the routine.

Antonia had met some of the greatest comic minds in entertainment and Chuck was inferior to none of them. She laughed herself to tears at one point, being brought back to reality for only a brief moment when she used little fair-skinned hands to wipe her eyes.

In spite of herself, Phoebe was really enjoying Chuck's stories too. For her the experience was like hearing a joke that you knew you shouldn't laugh at but couldn't help it, not even if you shut your mouth and plugged your nose. She hated people trying to cheer her up more than anything, but by six o'clock she was in a mood that was almost amiable. It was this, in fact, that led to a very important realization.

"Look at that smile," Chuck teased Phoebe gently, "you look like a mailman at a bulldog's funeral!" Phoebe scowled with effort.

"Wow!" Antonia laughed, "You got Jess to smile? That's real talent. Have you ever considered doing comedy professionally?"

"Sure," Chuck replied, "either that or male modeling."

The others chuckled. Julie's mouth slanted downward for a moment. "Speaking of people who don't usually laugh," Julie said, "when I got to the restaurant today Stanley Hobbes was blacked out behind the back door. I had his dad come get him. I've never seen somebody so depressed."

This sobered Chuck quickly and thereby the company. He nodded slowly. "Yeah, poor guy," Chuck said, "I don't know him well, but I know he's never been in a great place financially. Having a son with health issues probably doesn't help his stress level, either." Suddenly his eyes lit up with an epiphany. "You know what else?" Chuck said with rising excitement in his voice, "Stanley was having one just when that screwy thing happened with our brains."

"Having one what?" Dale asked.

"A seizure," Chuck answered. He stood up, taking stock of each of their expressions before settling on Jim. "You don't think that's what caused it, do you?"

Phoebe breathed a sarcastic laugh. "Like maybe your waiter had a magical seizure?" she mocked. Antonia glared her back into polite silence.

"Well, why not?" Julie offered in dignified defense of her husband's suggestion, "Aren't we beyond realistic explanations at this point? Besides, we don't have any other ideas."

"Couldn't hurt to ask Beaker what he knows," Jim submitted, standing up and reaching for his phone, then realizing that it was Axl's phone in his pocket and not his own. He appraised Chuck. "You got Leroy Hobbes's number?"

"I do," Julie volunteered, taking out her phone. A lot of people had Leroy's number because Stanley had given it to them. Stanley didn't have his own phone and sometimes he needed to get ahold of his dad.

The others waited in silence as Julie made the call. "It's ringing…Leroy Hobbes? Hi, how are you doing? This is Julie Hocum—Julie from Hometown Inn? Yeah, that's right. Hey, I was just calling to see how Stanley was doing and was wondering if I could come see him…Oh, really? I'm sorry to hear that. Well, maybe I'll swing by there sometime tomorrow to check on him, would that be alright?...Thanks so much, I promise I won't be there long. See you then!"

She hung up. "Leroy said he's still sleeping it off."

"Tomorrow, then?" Jim asked.

"Tomorrow," Julie repeated.

CHAPTER ELEVEN
ATLAS RANCH

Jim Boyd's ranch sat on twenty acres. Less than half of it had ever been cultivated, and all of that was within sight of the ranch house. Now most of the cultivated land was overgrown with wild native grasses and sagebrush. Dirt trails cleaved their way through the scrubland toward the hillier, more forested part of the acreage. Beyond that, past the edge of Jim's property, the hills became mountains, and beyond the mountains, sky.

Most of the property was left the way God had made it—which was how Jim liked it. Of course Jim used his big riding mower to cut a comfortable barrier between his house and Mackenzie's annual brush fires, but by and large he preferred the natural look of his landscape. He wanted to have claim to part of the wilderness, if only to know that it would always be kept wild. Hired help would be spending the next few days widening some of his trails for four-wheelers, but they were not to disturb any of the trails beyond the first trees. Those trails were narrow and meandering, letting the roll of the land dictate their course. Those trails were for horses and riders travelling a pace that would let them appreciate the beauties of nature: clear air, tall trees, and a million secret lives that advanced so subtly that most people never witnessed one moment of them.

Such was Jim's romantic, almost poetic view of the world. He appreciated most things the way they were, even if they were flawed and, in some cases, *because* they were flawed. To Jim, imperfection was one of the charming realities of life and especially of life in the West. A stunted tree in bloom or a fruiting tree leaning from a winter's burden of snow were monuments to every person who'd pushed forward in the face of adversity. A rugged trail might need care, but it also had stories to tell—footprints and scat of all kinds, ruts left by burdens dragged through the mud, pocketknives dropped by careless travelers. Why, even his cultivated land, left for grass and weeds to claim, was teeming with life and beauty. Jim had a talent for seeing the good in everything.

As such, Jim had no apprehensions about allowing a motley collection of strangers to stay at Atlas Ranch. He was glad to perform one of the most basic Christian duties: to love his fellow human beings. He planned to help them as far as his resources would allow. Still, he knew it wasn't an ideal group. After less than a day in one another's company a whole system of conflicting personalities was becoming apparent: Dale was suspicious of all of them and consequently was not well-liked by any of them. He kept silently to himself most of the time and was wary of personal questions.

Axl stayed close to his uncle and, to a lesser degree, Chuck and, to an even lesser degree, Antonia. Of Dale and Phoebe he was extremely wary, especially of Phoebe. They all were.

Antonia was preoccupied with her million unmet expectations and was constantly on edge in anticipation of Phoebe's sarcasm and threats. She also watched Phoebe like a hawk, ever protective of the body she'd left the girl.

Phoebe, of course, had made it clear that she didn't particularly like any of them, and for each she had consciously conceived different reasons: Dale's apparent stupidity and uptight demeanor, for example. She hated Chuck for being popular; she hated Jim for being nice. She hated Axl for being a crybaby and a teacher's pet to Jim. She also hated that he was prettier than her even though he was a boy. She'd never felt beautiful and resented beauty in others as much as she resented talent, wealth, and popularity. These were just some of the injustices that "average" people were condemned to from birth.

For that reason she hated Antonia most of all: famous, rich, confident, glamorous, athletic. Still, all of those reasons still seemed pretty until Antonia had beaten her up. Now Phoebe felt justified.

Jim was confident they'd all get along once they got used to each other, but still he hoped they wouldn't all be stuck together for that long. He wasn't looking forward to that evening when they'd be back at the ranch, making plans and decisions and sleeping arrangements. He knew it would be conflicts, not capacity, that would complicate bedroom assignments.

Atlas Ranch had more than enough room for all of them. It was composed of four buildings—the ranch house, the guest house, the barn, and the shed—arranged in a semicircle around a large unpaved parking area.

The ranch house was a large one-level house with three bedrooms and two bathrooms. The bedrooms had five beds between them which, when combined with the number of beds in the guest house, were perfect for small retreat groups. It also had a spacious common area with an adjoining kitchen, where the strangers had had their meeting that morning. It was a beautiful house, one worth living a life and then dying in. Jim and his wife had both contributed to the design and it looked like a dream when it was finished: a wraparound porch with old-fashioned posts and rails; white wooden siding with a black roof and blue trim; big windows with curtains, and lots of them. They'd planned on filling their three extra bedrooms with children—that's why they built the guest house.

The guest house had been one story as well, but Juan had been adding another level. Even with the other level the guest house was small, adding two more small bedrooms of two beds each, a kitchenette, and a bathroom. It matched the ranch house in color, style, and comfort.

The barn was the tallest and most spacious building at Atlas Ranch, serving also as a stables, a garage, a storage area and, if necessary, another sleeping area. It had a roomy loft that Jim had often said he'd gladly move into if nobody minded him coming to the house to use the bathroom and the kitchen. Beneath the loft had lived a number of different animals over the years, but now all that remained was Jim's collection of eight beautiful horses.

The shed was the smallest building by far, but was still large for a shed. Its shelves and hooks had never wanted for tools and supplies, though the ranch's use had altered the variety from time to time. It sat between the ranch house and the barn. It was conceivable that somebody could have slept in there, too, if they didn't mind voles and spiders.

Naturally, the group favored the seven beds of the ranch house to any of the other choices. Dale had suggested all of them sleeping in the big common area together so they could keep an eye on one another but Antonia said she refused to let Phoebe sleep on a hard wooden floor in *her* body—especially with the possibility of being in a movie the next day!

They were a bed short for each to have their own so Jim offered to give Axl the double-width bed in his own bedroom while he slept on the floor. Axl didn't argue. By then he was weary from the long day of trauma. They all were. Jim gave everyone a brief orientation of his property, reviewed the rules they'd all agreed to, and offered a few final words of encouragement before releasing his guests for the evening.

Antonia and Phoebe were the first to leave the room. Their luggage was in Antonia's Porsche, and in a single trip they brought in Antonia's three suitcases and Phoebe's backpack. Nobody had said it, but it was generally understood that each person's counterpart would be their roommate. "Which room is ours?" Antonia asked Jim.

"The one on the end," Jim said, "I'd offer you mine but there's only one bed in there." Antonia led the way into one of the modest, attractive rooms, laying her luggage on the bed and then immediately shutting the door behind Phoebe. Before Phoebe had even laid the other suitcase on the bed, Antonia was putting Phoebe's $1000 per diem to use.

"Listen," Antonia said quietly, but with gravity, "as much as I hate it, you're going to have to be in charge of all the embarrassing stuff. My body needs to be bathed and groomed and dressed and all that stuff just like anybody else. I'm gonna give you some guidelines, and then I'm gonna trust you to do that stuff. Can I trust you, Jess?"

Phoebe gave a smile and nod of forced pleasantness, one designed to magnify the awkwardness of the request. Antonia drew breath anxiously. "I want to make sure we get plenty of sleep tonight so we're going to do a super abbreviated version of getting ready for bed. But listen, I don't ever want to hear anything about my body. Observations, rude questions, smart remarks…"

"Rude questions?" Phoebe broke in with mock offense, "Smart remarks?"

"Just keep them to yourself, got it?" Antonia concluded. Phoebe smiled smugly and nodded.

Antonia unzipped one of the suitcases and flipped it open. She was a woman who loved sportswear—that much was clear—and bright eye-catching colors. Her wardrobe used the palette of a florist's shop where they fed the plants with electricity instead of water. There were intense indigo shades of lobelia, exciting celosia oranges with their characteristic rosy tints, overwhelming delphinium blues, and bromeliad reds so profound they were almost poetic. Their effect was magnified by backdrops of flat elemental shades—silvers and slates and ebonies and bronzes and ivories. Phoebe was stunned for a moment with jealousy, but finally broke her silence with, "Wow! Do you ever *not* dress like a Nike ad?"

"Try the other suitcase," Antonia insincerely invited as she handed Phoebe some pajamas, which in this case were shorts and a tank top. "Just go get dressed."

The TV screamed an anthem of destruction. The commercial was a seizure-inducing 60-second montage of gunshots, explosions, and reckless driving. An intense, dark-sounding voiceover recited a fill-in-the-blanks shoot-em-up trailer narration, an occasional reprieve from the cacophony of Wilhelm screams, machine gun reports, and abruptly-censored blips of dialogue.

Its hero was a muscle-bound man with a crossbow mounted between the handlebars of his Harley. Between his low gruff voice and the cigar perpetually clenched in his teeth, it was a wonder the movie didn't have subtitles. Little of the plot could be gleaned from the trailer other than that the hero had a goal of some sort that could only be accomplished by shooting lots and lots of bad guys and blowing up lots and lots of buildings.

"From the visionaries who brought you *Pop Goes the Uzi* and *Chainsaw Paladin*," the voice advertised, "comes a movie so 'rated R' that your parents won't let you see it until you're forty: *Kill, Drive, Kill*." The military-stencil title appeared as a 360-degree camera spin orbited a flaming jeep in slow-motion freefall.

"Can you believe movies these days?" Dale said, fidgeting.

"Sure ain't *The Brady Bunch*," Jim responded with a chuckle. Axl remained silent; the movie looked really cool to him.

Dale usually watched TV to unwind but tonight it wasn't doing much to ease his tense mood. Jim had suggested they take their minds off things by working on one of his puzzles but Dale and Axl both admitted that putting a puzzle together would only frustrate them.

"How about we turn this garbage off?" Dale said, "Axl, change the channel."

"It's not garbage!" Antonia exclaimed as Axl flipped to a different channel, "I'm in that one!" She was leaning against the doorway behind them, waiting for her turn in the bathroom.

Dale turned, wide-eyed with surprise. "Really?"

All eyes were on her. She suddenly felt very self-conscious. She shrugged a shrug of resignation. "It was just a cameo." The bathroom door opened. Antonia escaped through it as Phoebe took her place.

"What are we watching?" she asked.

"*Hogan's Heroes*," Jim answered with a grin as he squinted at the screen.

"What?" Phoebe returned with a raised eyebrow.

"You know: Sergeant Schulz, Colonel Klink," Jim returned with an encouraging tone. Phoebe raised the other eyebrow. "'I know no*thing*, I see no*thing*!" Jim quoted in an exaggerated German accent.

Phoebe cast another glance at the TV. "No, sorry," she said sarcastically, "I was born in the 21st Century." She looked out the window. Chuck and Julie were on the front porch, their arms folded and heads bowed, muttering softly. They were praying. Julie had thought it best that Chuck stay on the ranch until a plan was made to reverse the transference. Chuck had agreed. They'd been saying their goodbyes and were finishing the evening as they always did, by praying together. After their "amens" they embraced lovingly.

Phoebe noted tears in Julie's eyes. For a brief moment a feeling of sympathy visited Phoebe's heart, but it was fleeting. Sentimentality made her feel weak. Too many adults had used it influence her, control her, change her mind. Sentimental thoughts made her second-guess running away even when she knew she was in the right. She replaced the thoughts with more sarcasm.

Chuck walked in soberly as his wife drove away. "Prayers working yet?" Phoebe teased carelessly. Chuck sighed wearily and left the room. All eyes were on Phoebe. "What?" she demanded.

Dale averted his eyes, then Axl. Jim stood up casually, took a few steps toward the door, and then said to Phoebe in a low voice, "Let's go out on the porch."

"What for?" she asked defensively.

"To talk," Jim answered, nodding toward the open door. He led the way. As he waited for her at the far front corner of the porch, out of the view of any of his guests, Jim became more conscious than ever of his small size and prepubescent voice. He didn't care. This was his house, these were his guests, and as such he had an interest in their comfort and wellbeing. Phoebe joined him shortly, forcing an eye roll to mask her sheepishness.

"What do you want?" she asked defiantly.

"First I want you to lose the tone," Jim said firmly but not cruelly. Phoebe said nothing. "Seems like everybody's rubbing you wrong today," Jim continued, "You wanna talk about it?"

"No," Phoebe answered dismissively. "Can I go now?"

"Not until we talk," Jim said a little more assertively. "I know you know how to talk. Like the way you talked to Chuck just now—what was that about?"

"Cool it," Phoebe defended herself, "it was a joke."

"Jokes are funny," Jim corrected, "that was just kicking a man when he was down."

Phoebe knew what he was going to say, but this was the harshest tone she'd heard Jim use since meeting him. She stared at him, a little afraid.

"Am I not giving you the benefit of the doubt?" Jim asked, "Is this attitude just for today or do you always have a hard time playing nice with other kids?" She didn't answer. "Do you start a lot of fights like you did today?"

"Hey, hold on, I didn't start that fight," she defended.

"Maybe not," Jim cut her off, "but you sure as heck haven't been making yourself easy to be friends with, especially for Antonia. Do you know what a bad place she's in right now?" Phoebe didn't say anything. "How about Chuck, who can't even go home to his wife tonight, do you think he's having a good day?"

"Yeah?" Phoebe said, raising her voice and taking a step forward, "Well life isn't exactly swell for me either, Jim. For your information I'm going on six months of being homeless. Six months! You wanna talk about the last time I had a good day?"

"I'm sorry about that," Jim said without a pause, "but it's no excuse. There are a million reasons you could be homeless, Jess, but if you want to keep being friendless that's totally up to you." Phoebe shut her mouth and clenched her teeth angrily, holding back her tears this time. She'd had enough experience with being punished that being scolded didn't usually make her cry, but her emotions had worn pretty thin over the past week. Still, she refused to let anybody see her cry ever again. Jim didn't back down, nor would he regret her tears if they came. In fact, he raised his voice a little. "Let's start thinking about other people from now on, huh?"

"What do you want from me?" she murmured past the lump in her throat.

"I want you to grow up," he said. She didn't respond. Her eyes were fixed on her bare black feet. "Look at me," Jim said. She looked up. "You don't have to make everybody's bed in the morning, you don't even have to tell them they look nice—heck, Jess, I think you've lied enough for one day—I just want you to coexist. Everybody here is having a really bad time so just be a little civil, ok?" She nodded slowly, sniffling. "Ok," Jim repeated with a sigh, resting a hand on Phoebe's shoulder. He left it there for a while, waiting for Phoebe's breathing to return to normal. Then he went inside without another word, leaving her alone on the porch.

She stood there for nearly fifteen minutes in utter silence. Her thoughts were a tempest of remorse and anger, the former championing a course of repentance and restitution, the latter championing a course of embittered revenge. They were so equally convincing: she'd been so harsh and unfeeling to total strangers, and in turn they seemed so aloof to her own sufferings. She hated them for it. And now more than ever she hated Antonia: that perfect, rich, adored goddess. The whole world seemed enamored with her and Phoebe was suddenly given all her power. She could deal no greater blow to Antonia LeBlanc than to deprive her of the thing that she so worshipped: herself. Yes, she could take Antonia's body away from her. She wouldn't even need to sneak back inside for shoes—there was a discarded pair of dirty work boots at the foot of the porch. She scowled as she put them on.

Phoebe became so compelled by the idea that it was almost blinding. She took step after step guided not by sight but by bitter thoughts. She was within twenty yards of the forest before she realized she'd left the light of the porch. She was so close. To be on her own again, free—just as she'd wanted before. She stared hard at the ominous black trees. They were a wall of warning. Phoebe did not heed.

No sooner had she taken a single deliberate step forward before a harsh high voice commanded, *"Don't!"* Gasping, Phoebe looked around. There was no one. She leaned toward the woods again, only to see what happened. The voice repeated itself. There was no one. The voice was in her head.

CHAPTER TWELVE

THE BOY

Axl's parents Skype-called him every evening at 9 p.m. After their experience with Eric Lopez earlier that day neither Axl nor Uncle Jim had much confidence in Jim's ability to act like Axl. He did have the benefit of looking like the boy and he knew quite a bit about him, but he couldn't totally cover up his accent nor imitate the boy's youthful spark and talkativeness. They'd keep the call short, they decided, with Axl there the whole time to help out if needed.

Axl had a few minutes before 9 o'clock so he started gathering his things from his room to move them into the master bedroom. Chuck and Dale waited patiently for Axl to clear out the messy room. He hadn't yet learned the nuances of being a gracious guest. His bed was unmade, his dirty clothes lay in disarray all over the wooden floor, and debris from snacks dusted the bedsheets like confectionary sugar. Axl also realized he'd left a few things out in the open that were even more embarrassing than dirty underwear: toys.

He didn't like being thought of as a "little kid" especially now that he was thrown into such an adult situation, but the small assortment of action figures, Legos, bouncy balls, and old-school Gameboy games weren't helping. Looking like Uncle Jim boosted his confidence. He was everything he'd dreamed of being: tall, lean, muscular, mustached. He looked great. He hadn't anticipated all of Uncle Jim's discomforts, though: achy joints, achy back, and toenail fungus. Jim had taken him aside at one point to orient him to the different medications he was on. There were four. Axl had never considered that even cowboys wear down.

The more time Axl spent as Uncle Jim the more he realized that he was better suited to be a young boy on a ranch than an old cowboy on a ranch. He was amazed how much duller Uncle Jim's senses were and how much he missed out on.

Like the fact that Atlas Ranch always smelled strongly of hay. It probably always had, but he was sure Uncle Jim wasn't aware of how pleasant and profound the scent was. Colors seemed so much duller through Uncle Jim's eyes. Every spring Uncle Jim would replant the garden beds around the house exactly the way Aunt Jess used to—it was his tradition. She'd had an eye for color: silvery wormwoods and emerald Mugo pines and zinnias of every vibrant hue. All of them seemed so washed out now. It also suddenly occurred to Axl that he'd never seen Uncle Jim run much. He used to think it was because it's hard to run in cowboy boots, now he was sure it was because of his achy knees. There were few things Axl loved better than to run through the tall grass at the edge of the property with Brodie, chasing rabbits and foxes and snakes. He'd ruined three pairs of socks that summer from getting too many "stickers" in them. Now he knew that this was a young man's game.

Axl threw all his things in his big suitcase unceremoniously while Dale and Chuck stood in the doorway. The suitcase was so big he couldn't carry it as a scrawny fourteen-year-old, he could only roll it on its awkward little wheels. Now he hefted it with ease.

Dale eyed the bed critically. "Aren't you going to take those crumbs with you, too?" he asked. Axl's ears burned with embarrassment.

"Nope," Chuck cut in, flopping down on the bed, "those are for me in case I get snacky." Axl smiled, relieved. He turned to go but Chuck called him back. "Don't forget Chewie," he said, pulling a forgotten Chewbacca figure out from beneath the sheets.

Axl set his suitcase down in the master bedroom with a couple of minutes to spare. The closer it got to 9 o'clock the more anxious Axl became. It wasn't because he thought his parents would realize he and Uncle Jim had switched brains—why on Earth would they think that? It was because he was afraid they'd find out about some of the other things he'd gotten to do on the ranch.

Axl usually did his Skype calls without Uncle Jim in the room so it was easy to omit the parts he thought Mom and Dad would disapprove of. Of course Uncle Jim knew not to tell them about his teaching Axl how to use a handgun—he'd made Axl swear under penalty of death to keep it a secret—but there were other things.

"Uncle Jim," Axl said, toying nervously with the triangular coin on Uncle Jim's keychain, "can we talk for a minute?"

"Sure," Uncle Jim replied, "but make sure it's just a minute. You're parents are gonna call any time."

"Okay, so here's the thing: remember how I told you we have a riding lawn mower at home and that I could mow your wildfire barrier for you?"

"Yep."

"Well I lied. That was my first time using one and I don't think Mom and Dad would like it if they found out."

Jim's squinted eyes widened. "Oh. Well maybe we'll just keep that between us, then. Anything else?"

"I'm not supposed to eat Starbursts," Axl admitted, "they're bad for my braces."

"You told me there wasn't anything you weren't allowed to have."

"Well, basically," Axl rationalized hastily, "I can have anything except Starbursts. Well, and nuts. And jerky. And soda pop. And—"

"Crying out loud, Axl, you've had all that since you've been here—and a whole bag of Starbursts to yourself!"

Axl's open laptop sang with the tone of an incoming Skype call. Uncle Jim gave him a hard squinty stare. This evening had been full of children who needed rebuking. "Axl, it's beneath you to lie to me and it's worse to lie to your parents."

"I know," Axl pleaded, "just please don't tell them about the mower!"

"Are they going to ask?"

"Yeah, probably," Axl admitted.

Uncle Jim seemed upset. "I won't tell them," Uncle Jim told him, letting the call keep ringing, "but you and I are gonna have a long talk one of these days."

He answered the call and all at once saw Axl's parents and his own reflection staring back at him. He tried to widen his squinted eyes.

"Hi, Axl!" his parents greeted in unison.

"Hi!" Jim greeted back.

"Is that your Uncle Jim behind you?"

"Yep, that's him alright," he smiled. That moment Jim became very distracted by the fact that *he* was lying to Axl's parents. Kind of. Virtue suddenly seemed very complicated.

"Howdy, Ryan," Axl greeted his father. It was a fair impression of Jim's accent, but the "howdy" was a bit much.

"Nice hat, Axl" Mom complimented. Jim forgot he was still wearing his cowboy hat.

"Thanks."

"What have you been up to today?" Dad asked with a yawn.

Jim thought hard about how to answer the question. "Well, we got some guests today. They're friends of Uncle Jim's."

"Is that one of them behind you?" Mom asked. Chuck was standing in the door.

"Sorry to interrupt," Chuck said. "Is there some way to open the window in our room?" He was looking at Jim when he asked the question, which confused Axl's parents.

"Yeah, I'll show you in a second," Jim replied, "right after we're done with this call."

Chuck looked into the screen, "Hi, Axl's parents," he smiled before leaving the way he came in.

"Wow!" Dad exclaimed, "That guy looks just like Don Knotts!"

Stanley awoke in the middle of the night. He was startled, disoriented. He felt weak and sick and confused. Then all at once it came back to him—Hometown Inn, the seizure, now his bedroom. His breathing gradually slowed as his eyes adjusted to the darkness and he found himself surrounded by familiar things: his dresser, his clothes, his stuff. Little curios he'd happened upon during his many walks sat in small collections throughout his messy room. It was hot. He wouldn't have felt up to getting out of bed, but his fan was just close enough to turn on. He collapsed back into his pillow as the humming breeze soothed him. Already his eyelids were heavy again. He was entering the twilight zone between consciousness and sleep.

The eerie voice came into his mind again. *"Stanley,"* it said urgently, *"Stanley, what happened?"* Stanley stopped breathing. A horrified lump swelled up in his throat so quickly that he almost threw up. *"Stanley, what happened to you today? At the Inn?"*

In a nightmarish torrent all his memories of the aliens came flooding back to him: the huge triangular spaceship and its arsenal of otherworldly lights and sounds; its luminous interior, so like a morgue with its pale unembellished walls and cold metal examination tables; the alien's mirrored exoskeleton with its distorted reflection of

Stanley's sunken face. The scar on the back of Stanley's neck seemed to burn as the microchip betrayed all of his secrets to the extraterrestrial scientists.

"Please, talk to me, Stanley," the voice urged. *"We're trying to help. We don't understand what happened, Stanley."* Stanley looked frantically around the room, then mustering whatever strength he had left he rolled himself off the bed, flopping heavily to the floor. He stared eagerly underneath the bed, but there was nothing there but more mess.

"Where is that stupid cat?" he grunted to himself, and then closing his eyes he focused. He focused as hard as he could. He focused until his thoughts drowned out the strange voice, scanning the house for his cat.

CHAPTER THIRTEEN

FRIDAY

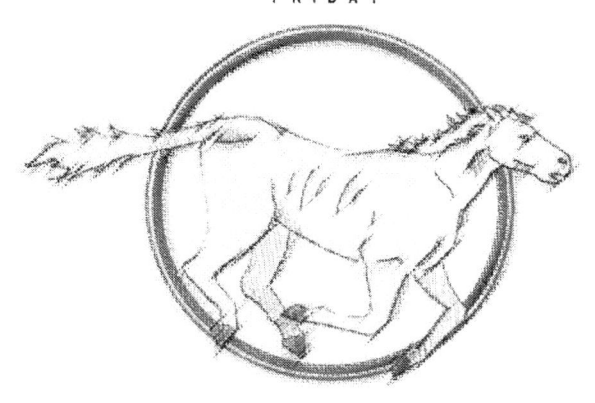

Jim was usually the first one up in the morning. Even the morning after the incident, when he didn't feel inclined to be more productive than watching the news, he still got up at six. He was surprised when, at six thirty, Antonia and Phoebe walked through the front door, evidently back from a run.

"Good morning!" Jim appraised them with obvious surprise.

"Wrong," said Phoebe without pausing. She disappeared into the bathroom.

Antonia took a seat near Jim and started unlacing her shoes. She was still slowing her labored breaths and her freckled face was red and sweaty. Still, after having had a shower the night before and now dressed in some of the fighter's attractive (if oversized) exercise clothes, the teenager looked a world better than when Jim had first seen her.

"How'd it go?" Jim asked.

"Not bad," Antonia answered, "I mean, not that good, but not bad. That girl didn't leave me a lot to work with."

Jim chuckled. "I'm amazed you were able to talk her into it."

Antonia smiled. "Which part? Exercising or getting up at five?" She cast a glance at the closed bathroom door as the shower began to hiss. "And you know what? She wasn't all that mean today."

"I figured she wouldn't be," Jim said matter-of-factly. "Yesterday was a rough day and I think sleep did us all a lot of good."

"Yeah," Antonia said absently, distracted by the TV. The word "Philadelphia" in the headline had caught her attention. Jim followed her gaze. It was another story about "Philadelphia Superman."

"You heard of this guy?" Jim asked.

"Only as much as anybody else who watches the news," Antonia replied. "Philadelphia Superman" had been the hot story for over a week. A three-day hostage crisis in a big commercial building in Philadelphia had ended when an unidentified hero leaped from a neighboring building, broke through a window, and took out all five gunmen unarmed. On-site SWAT teams, for all their famous promptness, could not get to the room before the hero disappeared back out the way he came in. Phone camera footage of his entrance, security camera footage of the skirmish, and professional news footage of his amazing exit became record-breaking viral videos the day they were filmed.

"How on Earth does somebody jump that far?" Antonia said, captivated by yet another review of the shot of Philadelphia Superman leaping from one building to the next. It looked even more remarkable in slow motion. It was nothing short of superhuman: the colossal leap, the agile escape, the incredible speed he used in the fight, not to mention his apparent indifference to all the shots taken at him by the gunmen. Many who watched the video said they'd simply missed, but several reviews of the video suggested that the bullets struck.

"Must be one heck of an athlete," Jim observed, then joked, "Can't you jump that far, Antonia?"

Antonia didn't seem to notice Jim's joke. She rarely had an opportunity to really consider the news, even when she got the chance to watch it. For the first time the incredible nature of the scene was sinking in. Antonia's life was so consumed by her career and all that went with it. She'd chosen it, of course, and she enjoyed it, but every so often she'd realize that the rest of the world was happening without her. "Philadelphia Superman" could be huge—historic, even. She'd have so little to say someday when her grandchildren asked her what she remembered about it.

"I don't get it," Antonia mused. "First there's this Superman guy, then this weird thing that happened to us at the restaurant. Did real life reach its expiration date?"

"Freaks you out a little, huh?" Jim asked.

"Yes and no," she said. "I'm not necessarily afraid of things I don't understand, but sometimes I wonder if I should be. And it's not just this, you know. There are a lot of crazy things happening, things that have never happened before. Normally I just accept it and get on with my life, but stuff like what's happened to us—I mean, do you realize there's a good chance we might never recover from this?" She paused as the gravity of her own words sank in. "I guess I always just took my understanding of the world for granted."

"Maybe," Jim said, "and maybe I've been thinking the same thing. But you know what I've decided? There's no reason not to be optimistic about it. This Philadelphia Superman doesn't make sense, but he's a good thing. Maybe this thing that happened to us will turn out to be a good thing too."

"I sure hope so," said Dale from behind them. He'd entered the room without them noticing. Both turned around to look at him. "I know, I know," Dale went on, "I got it wrong. We didn't sleep it off after all."

Breakfast at Hometown Inn was a great relief for all of them. Chuck had offered it all for free, so there was one less thing to worry about. It also did Chuck a lot of good to see his wife smiling, working and happy. She and her two helpers ran the restaurant just fine on their own. The helpers, of course, had no idea about the bizarre goings-on. They figured the group was all friends of Chuck's, which was true.

Hometown Inn's menu had just what was needed to put each of them in a good mood. That is, except for Phoebe. After Jim's rebuke the night before Phoebe had finally resolved to be a little more reserved if not kinder, but sometimes the resolution seemed too demanding. When Antonia told her that pancakes were forbidden for the foreseeable future Phoebe almost gave up on being nice *and* earning $1000 a day. "That's what I know how to eat," Phoebe protested, "what do you *want* me to have for breakfast?"

"Today you're going to have an egg white omelet and a chicken breast," Antonia said, "I'll even spoil you and let you have cheese on the omelet. And a piece of whole wheat toast, but no jam."

"How do you live like this?" Phoebe exclaimed. "What am I having for lunch?"

"Probably a big salad with walnuts and more grilled chicken," Antonia answered while studying the menu. She wondered if it would be too cruel for *her* to have something less healthy. She hadn't had anything fried in so long…

"Ok, fine," Chuck interjected, impersonating Phoebe, "but when you say 'salad,' how 'salady' are we talking? Because there's potato salad, you know, and that's mostly mayonnaise and bacon. I could have pasta salad, which is mostly oil. Ooh! Or how about pistachio salad? That's mostly pudding and marshmallows." Everybody laughed, including Phoebe.

Hometown Inn had renewed normal business operations so breakfasters came and went as usual. They all must have wondered what the big mismatched group sitting together was up to. Once or twice somebody seemed to recognize Antonia LeBlanc in the group. Phoebe would simply look at them and smile with her perfect teeth.

Chuck's business was taken care of. Jim and Axl had made a phone call to Juan and the other workers and asked them all to work on widening and blazing trails that day. That would keep the workers making money while also keeping them away from the house. Dale had the day off work and Antonia's director and agent were understanding but anxious. But what could they do? She was Antonia LeBlanc. She wasn't exactly replaceable.

All in all, with as pleasant as the morning was going, this dire situation felt vaguely like a vacation for some of them. It wasn't until Jim suggested they head over to Leroy Hobbes' place that they were brought back to the sad reality of their plight. Julie offered to call ahead, but Jim worried that Leroy would come up with a reason for them not to come over. They needed to see Stanley today, no matter what.

Axl asked if he could ride in the Porsche but Antonia didn't want to be separated from Phoebe and there were only two seats. Jim offered to squeeze both the girls in the truck if Antonia didn't want to drive her expensive sports car down gravel roads. "Oh, trust me," Antonia said, "I'm not leaving my car anywhere in Nowheresville, USA. When you pay as much as I did for my car, you take it with you wherever you go."

"How much *did* you pay?" Axl asked.

"You wouldn't believe me if I told you," she replied.

He smiled admiringly, eyeing the spectacular car. He was having another fame fantasy. "What do I have to do to drive a car like that?"

"Make lots and lots of money," Antonia laughed, sliding into the driver's seat, "Be the best, work hard, meet the right people." She winked. "Not to mention get a driver's license."

"Being rich and famous must be awesome," Axl said.

"It does have its perks," Antonia told him, "but it's also really demanding—don't lean on the car, please…"

"Demanding like how?" Axl asked.

"Demanding like my life is work. When I'm not working out or competing then I'm in front of a camera. Even when I'm not filming a movie or doing a photoshoot people are taking pictures of me. That's why I always have to look amazing—I mean, not right now, of course, but normally."

"Geez, thanks," Phoebe murmured.

"Hey!" Chuck called out from the driver's seat of Jim's truck, "speaking of looking amazing, I'd like to get back to being my beautiful self. Let's get going, huh?" Axl took another covetous look at the sports car.

"Well, it's nice to look at, at least," he said.

"You've got time," Antonia said reassuringly, "just make the right goals and start working on them. What do you want to be when you grow up?"

Axl laughed and looked himself up and down. "I think I'm already grown up," he joked. Chuck honked for attention. Axl climbed in the truck.

Phoebe was surprised when, before pulling out of the parking lot, Antonia handed her the iPod connected to her car radio. "What's this for?" Phoebe asked.

"It's for you to pick a song," Antonia said. "That way you can't hate on what we listen to."

Phoebe was confident she wouldn't find anything worth listening to, but she was wrong. She was amazed by how eclectic Antonia's tastes were. She had everything from electronic dance music to Broadway soundtracks. Finally Phoebe happened upon an artist that took her by surprise. She selected a song.

"*This?*" Antonia said with obvious shock. "*This* is what you like?"

"Yeah, sure," Phoebe replied almost sheepishly, "why not?"

"Oh, I don't know, it's just so…upbeat."

Phoebe wasn't sure what to say. "Doesn't everybody like Mika?"

Antonia nodded, still surprised but satisfied. She turned up the volume. "Yeah, I guess everybody likes Mika."

The Hobbes farm was similar to Atlas Ranch in a few ways—it could only be accessed by going down a poorly-kept dirt road that branched off from an even more poorly-kept gravel road, it was south of town near the edge of the woods out of sight of any neighbors, and it had a shed of comparable size between the barn and the house.

Other than that, they couldn't have been more different. Atlas Ranch looked comparatively lavish and spacious, especially with its recent renovations, repairs, and fresh paint. The Hobbes farm looked more like the rural Idaho equivalent of a haunted house. Its small dilapidated barn and two-story house looked ghost-infested. Only the last tenacious streaks of paint still remained while debris lay scattered across the property. The wire mesh on the screen door had rolled off of the frame in one corner and there were holes in the lattice under the porch big enough for raccoons to crawl through. Wispy spider webs and the papery husks of wasp nests crowded together in the eaves. Bat guano bleached the floor of the barn. On every wooden surface, five-fingered fronds of Virginia creeper hung in curtains. It was a sorry-looking property to say the least.

The group recognized one of the trucks parked out front—it was Eric Lopez's truck, and he was just unloading his derelict horse to show to Leroy. The two men seemed surprised—not only to have unexpected visitors at the Hobbes farm, but that one of the approaching vehicles was a flashy white sports car.

Dust settled as the whole company exited the vehicles and approached the two ranchers. Eric turned his head just enough to keep the group in his periphery while casting a questioning glance at Leroy. Leroy was at a loss. It had been strange enough that Julie Hocum had asked to visit Stanley, but most of these people were complete strangers to the Hobbes family and Julie was not among them.

Axl, per Jim's instructions on the way over, shook hands with the two ranchers and addressed Stanley's father. "Morning, Leroy," he said in his forced drawl, "heard about Stanley. How's he doing?"

Leroy's suspiciousness could not have been more apparent had he voiced it. He eyed them unblinkingly, arms folded protectively across his chest. It wasn't an aggressive suspiciousness as much as it was an apprehensive suspiciousness. "I don't know," he answered, "he hasn't been up today." He looked the group over, his circular eyes unblinking. "Are you *all* here to see him?"

"We were there when it happened," Antonia chimed in. "It was pretty traumatizing. It would do us a lot of good to see him all better."

Leroy wasn't satisfied with the answer, but he didn't know what else to say. He pulled a cigarette out and lit it, too frazzled to be conscious of etiquette. "Well," he grudgingly allowed, "I'll go check on him." He turned toward the house and walked away without another word to any of them or Eric, who still stood holding the horse's reins.

Eric didn't seem to mind. In fact, he seemed quite preoccupied staring at Phoebe. Phoebe had gotten used to it by now. She figured anybody who wasn't staring at her because she was famous was staring at her because they'd never seen a black woman before.

"Are you Antonia LeBlanc?" Eric asked.

It took Phoebe a second to realize he was talking to her. "What? Oh, yeah, that's me."

He looked around at the others, curious why they didn't seem more excited to be in the presence of such a big celebrity. He kept his own voice subdued. "I saw you fight Rita Squires in Vegas a couple years ago. It was a very impressive fight."

Antonia started to say something, but stopped abruptly, clearing her throat. "Thanks so much," Phoebe smiled, remembering her resolution as well as her fee. "That must have been pretty cool to watch."

"I'm a big fan of yours," Eric added as he patted the horse, which seemed irritated. "I've been watching martial arts for years and I've never seen anybody close to as good as you. What are you doing in town?"

Antonia and the others were slightly nervous about how this conversation would go but Phoebe didn't seem worried. "That's top secret," she answered with a sly tone. "It's one of those 'I could tell you, but I'd have to kill you' kind of things."

"I'll bet you could, too!" Eric laughed. "You probably size people up wherever you go." Again he looked about to the others, this time wondering why they hadn't laughed. It was a somber group. They all seemed fixed on the farm house, waiting eagerly for Leroy's return.

Eric stood up a little taller. "What if you and I were in the ring? What would your strategy be?"

This question was outside of Phoebe's expertise. Antonia interrupted. "That's a beautiful horse," she blurted out, obviously not looking very closely at the horse. "What's her name?"

"*His* name is Old Jobe," Eric told the teenager, then added with half a grin, "you want him?"

"I've always wanted a horse," Antonia replied cautiously, "but my parents would be livid if I said yes."

"That's probably right," Eric said with a slight air of disappointment, "and this wouldn't be a great starter horse for you, either. Jim was just telling me yesterday how there's not much horse left in Old Jobe and I'd have to agree—poor tired old boy. I'll tell you what, though, he might not be much of an athlete but he's sure smart. He used to be a trick horse for the circus before I got him. The guy I bought him from said he could do all sorts of tricks—play chess, even."

"Wow!" Dale exclaimed earnestly. His exclamation was followed by another from Antonia, but hers was one of pain. A scraggly orange cat had approached the group silently, slithering around and between each of their legs and shedding its fur in tufts. When the cat reached the teenager it scratched her pale leg fiercely, hissed, and retreated through a hole in the porch lattice.

"Dumb cat!" Antonia growled as she clutched her ankle.

"Geez, what did you do to it?" Axl asked. "Step on its tail?"

"No, I didn't do anything!" Antonia said angrily. "It was totally unprovoked."

"Oughta put that darn cat down," Dale muttered barely above a whisper, "or in a zoo."

The screen door slammed shut and rebounded noisily. Leroy called out to them as he closed the distance: "Sorry, Stanley's still out."

Each expressed disappointment. Axl kept in mind that he was Jim and had to appear the de facto leader of the group. "Would you be willing to wake him?" he begged, trying to think quickly. "We'd all really like to see him."

Leroy seemed a little offended. These people came to his farm in their fancy cars unannounced, while he was busy, made absurd demands of him, and then didn't take "no" for an answer. They weren't even sensitive to the boy's condition. He shook his head and threw his hands in the air. "You must never have lived with an epileptic!" he said. "The boy's had a seizure; he can sleep all he wants. As for all of you, I don't know what you're really up to on my farm, but I'd just as soon have you get back in your cars and go back where you came from. You can see Stanley the next time he walks into town, no need to come out here."

A few people started talking at once—some to try to reason with Mr. Hobbes, others to apologize, and Leroy simply to cut them off. "Enough!" he kept saying, "Don't wanna hear it, don't wanna hear it, you're done here." The tumult ended abruptly when Old Jobe suddenly reared up, seized the reins from Eric's slackened grip, and charged toward the forest with an unexpected burst of speed. He nearly knocked Eric over. He left a hoarse whinny in his wake, disappearing behind the tree line before Eric could even call him to come back.

Nobody could explain why, but more than one of the six strangers felt sure that the horse's strange behavior was somehow linked with their condition. It was a bizarre, abstract impression, but a profound one. And more than one of them felt sure that they'd see him again.

Given their circumstances, it seems that every one of them would be diligently engaged in finding a solution to the problem that Friday afternoon, but that's not what happened. Jim, who was a doer and felt that the others were counting on him, spent most of the day "at the helm." Back at Atlas Ranch, in the common area, Jim kept a computer set up for the convenience of guests. He sat visiting website after website and reading article after article. Chuck, who didn't have a computer or smartphone of his own, sat behind him, sometimes reading a significant phrase out loud or making a suggestion for further investigation or telling Jim what he should type. In that way Chuck felt a little bit like a backseat driver but Jim didn't mind, especially since he knew that, as the only married person in the group, Chuck was the most eager to rectify the situation.

Axl used his personal laptop computer to do his own research. At least that had been his plan. Though he had fulfilled, in a way, his dreams of becoming a cowboy, he decided he wanted his own body back. His time as Uncle Jim had given him a deeper respect and understanding of his uncle, but he'd also gained a greater appreciation for himself. He missed his young and vigorous body, braces and all. He could stand being a kid for a little while longer.

But first he had to turn back into a kid. Axl had set himself up in the master bedroom with his laptop and snacks (enjoying nuts, candy, and jerky while he didn't have braces) and hoped not to come out until he'd found a solution. But having the form of an older man hadn't affected his boyish tendencies at all and more than half of his time was spent on Homestarrunner.com rather than on any helpful websites.

Dale knew he'd never get used to the oddity of living in Chuck's body so he, too, was eager for a solution. But he doubted he'd be any help in finding one. He was also a foreigner to the internet and, like Chuck, didn't carry it around with him. Dale was easily occupied by things around the ranch—animals, books, pictures, puzzles. He spent the bulk of his time attempting to advance the 1,000 piece puzzle that Jim, Axl, and Juan had been working on. He felt a little guilty not helping out with the search and so he thought it only right to advance one of Jim's other projects.

Every so often Jim would feel his pursuits becoming monotonous and would take a break to do some chore (like caring for his horses). Each time he'd also take a quick tour of the ranch to check the wellbeing of his guests. "How's that puzzle coming, Dale?" he asked.

"Not too good," Dale admitted. "It's been half an hour and I've only found a place for one piece. How do you stand it?"

Jim smiled. "It takes a lot of patience and a lot of not having anything better to do."

"Did you put together all of the puzzles around here?" Dale asked.

"Yep."

"I really like that one of the globe above the fireplace, Jim," Chuck interjected, "is that a nod to the ranch's name?"

"What do you mean?" Jim asked.

"Oh, you know: 'Atlas Ranch', and an atlas is a book of maps of the world, just like that puzzle."

Jim thought for a moment and laughed. "You know what? I had never made that connection before. I named the ranch after the Blue Atlas cedar, my favorite tree, and hung that puzzle in the main room because it was my favorite puzzle. I'd never once thought of the connection."

Antonia and Phoebe came in from outside just then, breathing hard and sweating. Their occupations of the afternoon had been perhaps the most surprising. Phoebe, upon learning of the Spartan diet she was bound to by contract, had offered to do another workout to justify eating "real" food for dinner that night. Besides, in spite of herself, she'd actually enjoyed their workout that morning, though she'd never admit it. She hated getting up early, but it was pretty fun exercising in a body that was used to it. Antonia was ecstatic at Phoebe's unexpected complaisance to fitness and took advantage of it while she could, notwithstanding the incredible soreness she already felt from their run that morning. Antonia had forgotten how painful exercise is when you're first getting into it, but she was used to working through pain. She took her counterpart out to the barn to take her through a martial arts-focused workout. Antonia was seeing herself perform from a perspective that had never been available before. Though her form was lacking she looked good! She was becoming more and more excited for her upcoming screen time.

Phoebe wandered over behind Jim and Chuck. "How goes the search?"

Jim sighed. "Not good. At this point I'm willing to believe there was a gas leak at the Inn and we're all in some sort of coma dreaming this."

Phoebe focused in on the screen. "You still use Internet Explorer? What are you, Amish?" Antonia cleared her throat threateningly. "What time is it?" Phoebe asked, trying to save face.

"About two," Jim answered.

"You're kidding me!" Phoebe exclaimed, turning toward Antonia. "Do you realize we worked out through lunch?! We must have been in that barn for three hours!"

"And it was a great workout," Antonia said, clapping a hand on Phoebe's muscular shoulder. "You should be proud of yourself."

"Sure, sure," Phoebe said, browsing the kitchen, "I'm a real champ. But if I'm going to survive til dinner I'm for sure going to need a snack."

"Good idea," Antonia agreed. "Do you have any nuts, Jim? Fruit? Whey protein?"

"I've got trail mix and jerky," Jim offered.

"That'll do," Antonia said. "You can have a handful of each, but pick the M&Ms out." Phoebe cast her business partner a sulking glance. Antonia returned it with a severe one.

Friday afternoon passed largely without incident. They ate dinner at Hometown Inn, where Phoebe ate a meal that, to her, was still a little dissatisfying, but to Antonia seemed indulgent. Friday evening ended a day of fruitless research, but the party was in better spirits than it had been the evening before. After the restaurant closed Julie came to see her husband, to offer encouragement, and to pray. There was little else to record. There was nothing to suggest the hope, deception, and peril that the night would bring.

CHAPTER FOURTEEN

THE HORSE

"Axl, wake up."

He did. He spent a moment getting his bearings, first remembering that he was not in his own room and then that he was not in his own body. He grimaced and swallowed hard.

"Axl, do you hear me?"

He looked all around the dark room. The digital clock glowed "1:07" in red. Who had spoken to him? It was a man's voice. He leaned over the edge of the bed and watched Jim's narrow boyish chest rise and fall steadily. He was fast asleep. The door was still shut tight and nobody was at the window. Axl sat back with his blanket draped loosely around him, waiting. "Yes, I hear you," he finally whispered.

"Axl, go out to the barn," the voice said again. Axl was petrified. The voice was in his mind. He didn't breathe. *"Do not be afraid. I'm going to help you."*

Axl was still worried, but the voice sounded like one he could trust. It was a strange voice—a weird, accented, elderly voice—but it sounded sincere and free of malice. Axl stood up slowly and cautiously, not sure whether he wanted anybody else to wake up. He slid his bare feet into boots, snagging a loose thread with the thick yellow nail of his big toe. He stepped to the front door, which he found slightly open.

Outside the scene was a jagged black mass of trees' silhouettes set against a luminous blue night sky. It was an unambitious scene, yet had a certain modest beauty that he had come to look forward to each summer: night times that never got very cool or very dark set to the lullaby hum of a million invisible bugs. It didn't seem like the kind of night anything unusual would happen. But then he heard Brodie whine. The collie was cowering under the porch.

Axl made every effort not to make any noise though he wasn't sure if it was out of courtesy or if he was trying to protect his secret. Regardless, he walked slowly and stepped carefully as his squinted eyes adjusted to the twilight. The door to the barn was ajar. Inside he found Dale, staring confoundedly at a tall white horse that faced him in the center of the barn. It was Old Jobe; there could be no mistake in the shadows that the dim light cast across his ribs. The dark muzzle and ashen hair set against the pale, worn-looking hide were all features unlike any of Uncle Jim's horses. Each of the horses in the stalls was a picture of health and fitness, from the tall Chestnut-colored horse named John Wayne to Jim's newest horse, an Appaloosa named Betty.

Dale looked startled and slightly embarrassed when Axl walked in, as if he'd been interrupted in committing a sin. "Dale?" Axl said.

Dale started to say a number of frantic sentences but none of them lived past five words. Finally he just opened his eyes wide (until they almost protruded as much as his true eyes) and nodded toward the horse. "You heard it too?" Dale asked Axl.

The pallor of Old Jobe's hide glowed blue in the twilight. His eyes were black and lustrous like marbles. Those eyes seemed different than before: he once had a look of alertness, now he had a look of knowing. *"Turn on the light,"* the voice came again in Axl's mind. He flipped the nearby switch. *"Now, follow me outside."*

Axl looked hesitantly at Dale. Dale stared back at him hard, as if his gaze could hold him in place. "He asked me," Dale said, stammering, "but I'm not doing it. I don't even know this guy." He waited, then Axl stepped decisively toward the door and Dale blurted, "What exactly is going on here, anyway?"

"I don't know," Axl told him. Jobe's stride was purposeful, but not fast. They followed him back outside, where he stood at the edge of the light spilling out from the barn door. He stared off into the blackness of the trees, ears twitching. Axl cast a glance at Dale, meeting Dale's concerned stare. Dale withdrew his eyes apologetically. They waited in silence for two whole minutes. "Who are you?" Axl finally asked the voice, directing his question at the horse.

"Jobe will suffice," the voice replied. *"What do you see?"* he asked the two of them, maintaining his fixed gaze on the edge of the tree line.

The two of them stared hard, searching. Dale drew breath fast and took a step back. A second later there was a rustle in the trees and, although only a fleeting blur, Axl saw it too: something moving in the woods. It was a silhouette too large and too misshapen to move with much stealth. With each step fleeing birds betrayed its presence, yet as it returned to monument stillness the figure was almost completely concealed by the trees and the darkness. Without the assistance of the light from the barn Dale and Axl wouldn't have been able to tell there was anything there at all, and even with the light the two men could make out only the vaguest details of the distant giant. The monster must have been nearly eight feet tall. It made no threatening advances and stood absolutely still, as if unsure whether or not it had been discovered. The horse turned away and took a few slow steps to another corner of the barn's beam of light. The two men followed, cautiously casting back at the shadow in the woods.

"Don't look back," Jobe said.

"What is it?" Axl asked.

"Its kind is called Orliak, a forest giant," Jobe answered. *"There will be others."* Dale swallowed hard. The horse turned around to face them and told them solemnly, *"They're very dangerous."* Dale swallowed again. Axl clenched his fists.

"What should we do?" he asked.

"Go and wake the others and bring them here," Jobe ordered.

Moments later all six guests were assembled in front of the barn, and not sleepily. Axl's urgency and the strangeness of his request had put them all on their guard. In his characteristic way Axl talked fast and excitedly, trying to respond to every person's questions at the same time, repeating himself and tripping over his unfamiliar tongue. These mannerisms were so fully Axl's that nobody once considered that Jim might have gotten his body back.

Phoebe's thoughts were full of curses, but she was compliant, hoping that Axl was rousing them because he'd made a promising discovery. She was perhaps most surprised of all when they were led outside to see a horse waiting for them in the center of the unpaved parking area. Jim actually looked past the horse and first noticed something that Dale and Axl had both missed: a veritable dam of trees and boulders had been dragged across the gravel driveway and now blocked the only way for cars to drive in or out of the ranch.

The voice entered all of their minds at once. *"I am Jobe,"* said the circus horse. *"I am here to help you."* Jobe was almost disturbingly calm. His head was raised attentively and he was still other than the occasional blink of his black eyes.

Phoebe, who had been searching for the source of the voice since coming outside, finally exclaimed, "No. Horses don't talk. This is stupid. Where is the voice really coming from?"

"You are free to choose to believe or not to believe," said the cerebral voice that all of them could hear, *"but if you want to live then you'll at least do what I say."* The snapping of branches and exclamations of birds seized everyone's attention at once. Few eyes were quick enough to catch a fleeting glimpse of the gigantic shadow's retreat. It was gone, but would not go far.

All eyes finally returned to Jobe. *"Atlas Ranch is being surrounded by Orliak giants at this very moment,"* he warned. *"They withhold their attack because of me."*

"What's an Orliak?" Chuck asked. The others started to speak over one another until Jim threw up a silencing hand.

"Beings from another time, another plane of existence," Jobe told them. *"They are extremely cunning, very strong, and very fast. Do*

not try to best them in speed or in combat: no earthly weapon can pierce their skin or break their bones."

"What do they want?" Antonia asked.

Jobe answered with gravity, as if the group would understand the import of his words: *"They are the servants of Stynaksz."* Simultaneously three of the group began to ask who Stynaksz was, but Jobe continued over them. *"He is a being you must fear and never trust. I cannot expect you to understand, and for now you don't need to. What you do need to know is this: you cannot leave Atlas Ranch, not tonight, not tomorrow. Help will come, but until then I'm the only one that can protect you. Nine giants guard the perimeter, and they will wait until one of you strays far enough away from me to kill you."*

"Who are you?" Antonia asked.

"I am Jobe," he repeated, *"and I am your protector. As long as I am at Atlas Ranch you need not fear, but it is absolutely essential that you remain here. Do you understand?"*

Each of them nodded, including Phoebe. She wasn't convinced, but she hadn't been planning on leaving the ranch anyway.

"Who's coming to help?" Jim asked, "Will they be able to change us back?" He asked this assuming that Jobe was familiar with their circumstances. He really had no reason to think this other than this night's miracle was equally as bizarre as Thursday morning's.

"Yes, I believe so," Jobe said, *"I am sorry for your condition. You've all been caught in the crossfire of an intergalactic war that's been going on for centuries. Those who are coming are on the good side. They will heal you and they will rescue you, though for a time they will need to take you away from here."*

"Take us away?" Chuck asked with desperation in his voice, "why?"

"What's happened to you makes you extremely valuable to Stynaksz. The knowledge he'd gain from experimenting on you could turn the war in his favor. He must not succeed. But with virtue in our favor, my comrades will reach us first. You need not fear them, or Stynaksz, or anything that could happen to your families while you are gone. There is promise on the horizon and you are but a part of it. Trust in me, stay on Atlas Ranch, and I will do all I can to keep the giants at bay." Then he turned and began to walk away from them back to the barn, as if weary of answering questions.

The group was confounded for a moment but Phoebe broke the silence. "That's it?" she exclaimed in apparent discontent. "Hey! Hey, Jobe, come back here! What do you mean they're taking us away? Where are we going? That's not enough, Jobe!"

The horse didn't acknowledge her but simply disappeared behind the barn door. Jim cast confused glances at the others and followed Jobe as far as the barn door. Inside the white horse was eating hay just like any normal animal. Jim closed the door quietly as Phoebe resumed her tirade, this time to the general group.

"Man, I am so sick of this *Freaky Friday* crap! None of this is real. Stuff like this just isn't real, got it!"

"You got any better ideas?" Antonia shot back accusingly.

"Plenty!" Phoebe growled, finally proposing the conspiracy theory she'd been putting together during Jobe's monologue: "We're all under some sort of mass hypnotism, get it? Or drug-induced alternate reality, I dunno, something like that. Then this whole bit about Jobe is just to keep us prisoner on the farm."

"To what end?" Antonia demanded amidst other objections.

"And how do you explain that voice inside our heads?" Axl interjected.

"There are about a million ways they could be doing that!" Phoebe pursued, speaking with increasing speed and volume. "Speakers, ventriloquism—heck, maybe it's just part of the hallucination. You know what I think, though? I think that that freaky little voice is some ventriloquist who worked at the circus where Jobe came from."

"What could he possibly want from us?" Antonia reiterated in aggravation.

"I don't know, maybe he's nuts," Phoebe ventured without a moment's hesitation. "Maybe we're all nuts! Anyone who believes all that stuff about Stynaksz and his scary monster soldiers out in the woods has got to be!"

"We saw them!" Axl protested.

"Did you really?" Phoebe demanded skeptically. "What did you really see? Did anybody else see anything?"

"I-I did," Dale stuttered clumsily.

"Great!" Phoebe said. "So Jobe has the testimony of a loser and a fourteen-year-old boy. Good for Jobe!"

All the others protested Phoebe's harsh words in unison. "Nobody cares what you think, you ugly little girl!" Dale burst. It was what he wished he'd said the last time she'd been cruel to him.

Phoebe held her head in her hands, slowed her breathing, and blocked out everyone's words just long enough to calm down. "I'm sorry, I'm sorry ok?" she apologized, looking at Dale in particular. "But you've gotta admit, there's something really weird going on here.

It feels wrong. I just don't think 'Jobe' is telling us the truth." The others were silent. "Does anyone?"

"I do," Axl said readily.

"Yeah, me too," Jim said. Naturally he would trust a horse. Antonia just gave a hesitant "yeah," and Chuck just nodded, preoccupied with how Julie would take the news.

"I don't get it," Dale said.

"What's there to get?" Axl said. "We're stuck here until help comes."

"What is help?" Phoebe pursued, "Who is help? Jobe was awfully vague. We're just supposed to barricade ourselves in the ranch house until we all die of starvation? Just because a horse told us to?"

"Well, a telepathic horse from outer space, yeah," Chuck said with an ironic smile. Phoebe did have a point, though. Having had only Axl for a guest and having eaten at Hometown Inn at least once a day all summer, Jim didn't have a lot of food stored up at the moment. Certainly not enough to sustain six people for more than a couple of days.

"What a zoo," Dale muttered.

"What about other people coming onto the ranch?" Axl brought up, approaching the situation from a more practical perspective. "Like Uncle Jim's workers or Chuck's wife?"

"I don't *want* my wife coming here with those monsters around," Chuck said.

"Or my workers," Jim added. "Besides, it's the weekend. They won't be back until Monday and I hope this whole thing will be cleared up by then."

"Yeah, or we'll be dead," Phoebe said sincerely, but with a tone of frustration. There was a long, solemn silence after she said this. It was Dale who broke it.

"So what do we do?" he asked.

Jim ran his hand through his dark hair in thought. He looked around, taking stock of the house and the barn and the guest house and the shed. He glanced back to the vacant gap in the trees where the looming shadow of the Orliak giant had once stood and then back to the comforting luminous crack in the barn door. He'd leave the light on in there. It would be like a night light for all of them. Jobe had seemed earnest. At any rate, Jim was certain they had nothing to fear that night. "For now," Jim finally said, "we sleep." He really did think it best.

"Not me," said Phoebe, "I don't trust that horse any more than I trust 'Stynaksz' or his 'giants'."

"You sure?" Jim asked encouragingly. "It might do you a lot of good."

"I'm too paranoid to fall asleep anyway," Phoebe reasoned. "You can all go back to bed if you want, I'm going to stay up and keep an eye on Jobe."

Dale, relieved by the idea, muttered a "thank you" and turned back toward the house with the others. Phoebe followed them as far as the porch, where she pulled up a rocking chair and wrapped her blanket tightly around her. The others returned to bed, save Chuck who called his wife immediately to warn her not to return to the ranch.

Antonia returned to the porch from the bedroom with a blanket draped about her shoulders like a cape. "I'll stay up with you," she said to Phoebe and pulled up another chair.

"Think I'll get lonely?" Phoebe mused.

"I think you'll get scared," Antonia smiled back. "Besides, if those monsters do attack, I'm the only one I trust to protect *my* body."

"No way!" Phoebe joked. "You taught me Kung Fu today. I'm a dangerous weapon now."

"I have to admit," Antonia said, "you're not as bad as most first-timers."

"I'm so flattered," Phoebe replied in her sarcastic way.

"When you get a compliment like that from an Olympian, you should be," Antonia said. Both grew quiet and drifted into eavesdropping unconsciously. Julie was not taking the news of her husband's increased peril well. Chuck wasn't a crier but one could always tell when he was disheartened. He reassured his wife in hushed tones and stood in a very private stance, keeping his elbows close to his body. The pangs of guilt came back to Phoebe as she remembered her unkindness toward Chuck the night before. A haze of apparent retroflection came over her as she and Antonia sat in silence waiting for Chuck's call to end. Finally, "I love yous" were said, reassurances were given, and Chuck followed his counterpart's example and went to bed.

"How long have you really been on your own?" Antonia asked unexpectedly. Phoebe didn't answer at first, and then Antonia tagged on, "Phoebe?"

Phoebe was taken aback. "How do you know that name?"

"Your driver's license," Antonia admitted. "I went through your backpack after you ran away from Hometown Inn yesterday."

It hadn't occurred to Phoebe that Antonia might have gone through her bag even though she'd had it with her. She was outraged at first: "You went through my backpack?"

"You went through my wallet."

Antonia's frank reply seemed to calm Phoebe, reminding her that she didn't have to get upset. "A little over a week," Phoebe finally answered solemnly. In Phoebe's fantasies of confession she was always impassioned and very in control. This was different.

"I figured it had been about that long," Antonia said.

"How come?"

"You just had so little with you: one set of clothes, a few snacks, a phone, a couple bucks. I figured you couldn't have lived off of so little for so long."

"Yeah."

A pause. "Why'd you run away?"

"None of your business." Phoebe's response didn't have the same poisonous tone she usually used. It was very matter-of-fact and mechanical. It took only a moment of thought before she realized that she actually did want to talk about it. "I wasn't happy at home," Phoebe confessed. "Nobody really liked me."

"I find that hard to believe," Antonia said, not intending to sound as sarcastic as she did.

"Look, if you're just going to make fun of me—"

"I'm not," Antonia interjected. "Sorry, I just meant that you seemed pretty bearable today. I'll bet before you ran away you weren't all that bad."

"Yeah I was," Phoebe said without a moment of hesitation. "I'm the oldest of five and I'm rotten enough for all of us. I'm always the one who starts the fights, always the one who skips out on chores, always the one who breaks the rules…"

"Says who?"

"My dad," Phoebe said. "The point is my relationship with my parents hadn't been the greatest anyway. So then a couple weeks ago we go to the public pool and they put me in charge of the two littlest. Not really my favorite thing to do at the pool, but I did it. After a while a few of my friends happened to show up and I got to talking to them for a couple minutes. Next thing I know there's shouting and lifeguards and my little brother Todd is coughing up water and they're calling the EMTs."

"Was he okay?" Antonia gasped.

"He ended up being fine, but it sure didn't do a lot to make my parents like me. I told them I was sorry; a million times I told them. And Todd. And I was. I'd never felt worse in my life, and I'd never done anything near that bad. But they didn't care. To them, bad kids are never really sorry."

"So you ran away because they were angry at you?"

"No. It just so happened that I had gotten my driver's license recently and my birthday was coming up. I've always dreamed of having my own car and I'd been saving up for it. Once things settled down about the accident at the pool I went to my parents and asked if they'd be willing to help me out with the car for my birthday."

"And they said no?"

"Did they *ever* say no! Anyways, it was a bloodbath. I ran away just after."

Antonia processed what had been said. Phoebe's story still didn't sound like grounds for running away, and it sounded like Phoebe was beginning to agree. Suddenly the fighter felt very sorry for the runaway. Phoebe had been living with pain. She must have been so stressed and scared and angry after all that time on her own, all that time letting her anger and shame drive her farther and farther away from home. What a desperate case. Had she been living off convenience store food? Had she slept in alleyways and parks for the past week? Had she been sleeping at all, with the image of her little brother drowning haunting her dreams?

"Have you ever thought about going back?" Antonia asked.

"Not really. Not until yesterday." This response hit Antonia hard. She was thinking of an appropriate response when Phoebe added, "Guess it doesn't matter now, huh?"

"What do you mean?"

"Well," Phoebe said, "I don't happen to trust Mr. Horse in there. Him and his weird voice and his nine giants. With all the freaky *X-Files* stuff that's happened in the past couple of days, I kind of see all of us ending up either in some lab or some unmarked grave."

Antonia was disturbed by how nonchalantly Phoebe's theory was voiced. Phoebe didn't exhibit the slightest bit of grief over her hypothesis. "What an optimistic thought," Antonia murmured. "So what's your plan, then?"

"Stay put I guess," Phoebe said.

"Really? Not run away?"

"What for? Where to? Besides, I've only got enough cash to last me maybe a day."

"Plus the $2000 I owe you," Antonia reminded her with a smile.

"Right," Phoebe smiled back. "And don't think just because we're friends now I'm going to forget about it."

CHAPTER FIFTEEN

THE BIRDS

Antonia and Phoebe talked for over an hour longer before finally falling asleep. Before running away Phoebe had never slept sitting up before and she didn't care for it. She eventually ended up curled in a fetal position on the porch. Antonia had done a lot of international travel and had had to get used to sleeping on airplanes. By comparison, Jim's rocking chair was luxurious.

They awoke to the sounds of clinking dishware and kitchen utensils. Jim and Chuck were making breakfast. True, Jim didn't have cellars bursting with food, but he had staples enough to feed them for a few meals. For breakfast he had bacon, biscuits, eggs, and gravy. Phoebe's special diet was ancient history.

Dale and Axl sat on the couch watching TV. Chuck and Jim didn't really need their help and they hadn't asked for it. Besides, Axl and Dale seemed shaken up from the events of the prior evening more than any of the others. The atmosphere of the house had sobered. It was less of tenseness now and was more of a despondent resignation. It was the calm before the storm.

The two women walked in groggily and then separated: Antonia to the kitchen to help Chuck and Jim; and Phoebe to the common area to lie down again. She had a headache and a backache and she exhibited all apparent signs of having slept on a hard wooden porch. Her coarse black hair looked lopsided and was dirty. Her blanket was wrapped raggedly around her.

"Anything I can do to help?" Antonia asked.

"You can open the window over the sink," Jim said. "It's getting pretty steamy in here."

Antonia did so. She examined the dreary morning scene. A thin layer of pale gray clouds was spread over the sky. The sun couldn't seem to break through the seamless blanket of gray. Old Jobe stood in the open dirt area in front of the house, perfectly still. If not for the slow inflating and deflating of his sides he might have looked like some sort of grotesque lawn statue. Antonia's attention was drawn away by sounds from the TV.

"What are you watching?" she asked.

"Cartoons," Axl said simply. "It's Saturday." He realized how childish he must seem and then added, "Didn't you watch cartoons on Saturday mornings when you were a kid?"

"Some Saturdays," Antonia answered.

"I still do sometimes," Chuck admitted. Phoebe watched Saturday morning cartoons religiously, but she didn't feel up to talking just yet.

Axl got up at the commercial break and went to the sink for a drink of water.

Antonia unconsciously took a seat on one of the tall kitchen stools as she kept her eyes fixed on the cartoon. "You know, Phoebe," she began, "I was thinking about some of those theories of yours last night." Phoebe raised her eyebrows acknowledging but still didn't speak. "I think you may be onto something—"

At that moment Axl let out an awful shriek. Everyone turned to see the cowboy flailing and whipping his head back and forth, making a thrashing black blur out of a mass gripping the back of his neck. Axl's voice was full of pain and fright: "Stop! Stop it! That hurts! Stop!" Staggering and leaning hard into the imitation-stone countertop he tried to beat the creature off with the mug he'd been drinking out of. After several disbelieving double-takes they could all tell what it was: a magpie.

The moment Axl had turned away from the sink it had flown through the window like an arrow, clutched the base of his neck with its talons, and began pecking and tearing at his nape with its sharp little beak. Even now as it suffered the blows of the mug it seemed determined in its efforts to bore a hole through the boy's neck. Jim and Chuck rushed over to help, though Jim's undergrown fourteen-year-old frame was too short to be of much help. Axl bent over almost in half and then finally knelt on the floor, still flailing as he tried to free his neck from the bird's grasp. Chuck and Jim did their best but the magpie kept their hands from getting a good grip by flapping its wings furiously as it dug, dug, dug into the cowboy's neck, blood flowing freely.

The attack seemed to last forever, especially for Axl, but less than a minute after the boy's initial scream the magpie beat its assailants off with its black and blue wings and flew back out the way it came in, disappearing behind the roof of the barn. It left a deep oozing gash in the cowboy's neck. By this time Axl was sobbing uncontrollably.

Jim grabbed a dish rag and handed it to Chuck, telling him to apply pressure while Jim ran to the medicine cabinet. Antonia, Dale, and Phoebe had all rushed into the kitchen and were clustered around Axl, staring on in shock. Jim returned presently with supplies.

"What on earth just happened?" Antonia exclaimed.

"It was a bird," Chuck answered, washing the bloody rag off as Jim worked. "It came in through the window and started attacking Axl."

"Why?" asked Dale. The front door yielded without anybody turning the handle. Old Jobe trotted in with a curious swiftness in his step. He'd heard the commotion from the courtyard.

"Yeah, why?" Phoebe echoed, directing her voice to Old Jobe.

The horse was silent at first, simply staring. All eyes finally fell on him save Axl's and Jim's.

"This was the first attack," Jobe said, his tone not totally confident. *"Stynaksz is more cunning than I'd given him credit for."*

"I thought you said you could protect us!" Phoebe shouted accusingly, pointing to the carnage on the back of Axl's neck.

"I can," Jobe responded, *"but I need each of you to be vigilant. Keep all the doors and windows closed, don't let anything in."*

"Yeah, like you!" Phoebe returned distrustfully, advancing on the horse. She seemed preparing to send him away by force. Jobe reared up and howled, sending Phoebe back stepping in retreat. As he howled, the window and all the cupboards slammed shut, glasses shattered, and the TV reverted to static, hissing with white noise. More than that, though, all six of the terrified humans could feel an unearthly reverberation, like waves of air. But they felt it in their metaphysical souls more than in their mortal bodies.

The horse stared at Phoebe threateningly for some seconds. *"Don't test me,"* the voice hissed, *"if some of you don't survive I'll still count it as a victory."* He stared her down unblinkingly, then slowly walked away backwards. The door closed without a touch.

Axl slowed his sobbing. Jim sighed. Dale was still holding his breath but didn't realize it. Phoebe turned to her companions.

"We're *his* prisoners," she said with conviction. "I don't care if none of you agree—I can feel it in my bones! I don't think half of what he told us is true and if anybody is really coming here I don't think they're going to help us. Maybe it's just like Dale says: maybe it's like we're in some sort of zoo. They're just watching us, messing with us, waiting for us to go crazy or kill ourselves or something! This is all wrong, every last bit of it." She slowed and her tone became more severe: "We die on this farm. Get it? If we don't leave, we're all going to die."

Phoebe didn't pursue it any further. She knew she'd made her point. Part of her wanted to put it to a vote: run for it or trust Jobe and hope for the best. But they'd probably die either way and she didn't want anybody's blood on her own hands.

The day continued with unparalleled tenseness. After their last encounter with Jobe the group was more divided between those who trusted him and those who didn't, but all were wary of him.

Escape would've sounded attractive to any one of them if there had been a realistic plan. But with monsters hidden in the woods, vicious birds in the skies, and with Jobe keeping watch, none of them felt that they'd make it very far. The prospect of being held prisoner in the house indefinitely suddenly made Atlas Ranch seem very small and shrinking, with barely enough oxygen to last them for that day.

At one point Jim quietly invited Chuck to his room. Jim asked Axl not to follow, but Axl insisted on not leaving his uncle. Out of earshot of the others Jim loaded his two revolvers, entrusting one to Chuck and keeping one for himself—"Just in case," he said. Jim didn't want Axl to feel like he wasn't trusted, but he assured his nephew that shooting bottles lined up on a fence post was nothing like shooting a distant moving target. Axl didn't argue.

Nobody dared challenge one another's actions. It was as if the atmosphere of that house was a gas leak that a raised voice could ignite. Phoebe was a stress-eater, as was Chuck. They both made frequent trips, almost unconsciously wandering into the kitchen and browsing the cupboards and refrigerator. Antonia never mentioned it once. She sat on the recliner reading a magazine she'd bought in an airport on her way to Idaho.

Axl sat close to Jim, trying not to think about the ugly wound in the back of his neck. It still stung and throughout the day Jim had to redress it twice. Chuck had cleaned up the gore in the kitchen, noticing without a second thought a tiny glint on one of the bloody rags. It had been the microchip that the magpie had torn from Axl's neck.

Jim, Axl, and Dale watched TV that day almost without ceasing. Jim's thoughts were on his endangered guests and uncompleted chores; Chuck's thoughts were on his worried pregnant wife. Antonia worried about a film project that couldn't go on without her and that was now more than two days behind schedule. Phoebe and Axl had passing thoughts about their families, wondering if they'd ever see them again. It was only Dale who was not totally miserable. As frightening and unpleasant as their situation was, its many novelties gave Dale the oddest suggestion of a thrill.

Nobody showered that day. They were all too afraid to be alone for any reason. Privacy was still generally respected, but many of them were even afraid to close the door all the way when they needed to use the bathroom. Social mores suddenly seemed so trivial. When Chuck asked "Jess" why Antonia had called her "Phoebe," she didn't even think it worth it to deceive him and the others further. She told them everything.

They found peace of mind in nothing. The prospect of death and fates worse than death suddenly made all of the dreams, pleasures, prejudices, and insecurities of their lives seem so silly and one-dimensional.

Antonia finished her magazine and tried to entertain herself with her phone and the TV show the others were watching. She felt so antsy. She needed to run or do jumping jacks or go outside or something. She noticed a windowed cupboard with board games on one shelf.

"Anybody want to play Scrabble?" she invited.

No one responded at first. Jim would've been happy to oblige, but Axl seemed to need him nearby. Jim raised his eyebrows at his nephew as if to ask if Axl wanted to play. Axl only grimaced.

"I'll play," Phoebe said, scooting from the couch onto the floor. Antonia sat cross-legged on the opposite side of the board.

Phoebe expected to win. She was good with words. Not that she cared to win, nor did Antonia. Antonia was competitive but under the circumstances she was just glad have something distracting to do.

Each drew seven tiles, then an eighth to decide who went first. No sooner had they done this than another invader dropped through the chimney. The bird landed heavily at the foot of the fireplace, bringing everyone to their feet with surprise. All of them scrambled across the room or behind furniture in terror of the little black magpie. It kicked the bag of tiles into disarray, giving a flap of its wings that sent a cold blue sheen glinting down its sleek, pointed feathers. The bird squawked at them as if warning them to keep away, and then to everyone's amazement it began arranging the scattered wooden letter tiles of the game.

One by one they brought themselves cautiously out of hiding, starting with Jim. What was the bird doing? It was making words: plain, meaningful, English words. The first it put together was "danger." Axl, who despite his attack earlier now leaned in closer than the other, recited the words as they appeared.

"*Danger*," Axl repeated.

"Yeah, no kidding," Phoebe whispered.

The magpie made another word. Its method was a bit of a balancing act but it moved with remarkable dexterity. "*Lies,*" Axl read with surprise, "what lies?"

Nobody said anything, but the bird seemed to hear and understand the boy as it made the next word: "Jobe."

"I knew it," Phoebe whispered.

"That's great, Phoebe," Chuck said impatiently. "Now what are we going to do about it?"

The bird cawed again in response to Chuck, and then wrote a final word.

"*Escape*," Axl read. Nobody said anything for many seconds. "Escape?" Axl repeated. "How?" The bird released a final knowing squawk and then disappeared back through the fireplace, leaving behind a puff of ashes. All six of them rushed to the windows at the front of the house. Jobe's back was fortuitously turned to them at the moment as he grazed. The barn door stood partially open and, as their magpie came into view of the windows, they observed the bird disappear into the barn. Three others followed, one at a time. Jobe never noticed. Just when all the spectators had grown almost too anxious to endure waiting for the bird's explanation, one final magpie entered the scene, carrying a writhing rattlesnake by the neck.

It dropped the serpent within feet of Old Jobe. The horse shrieked, reared, and retreated. For a self-proclaimed otherworldly guardian, Jobe suddenly seemed very vulnerable. The magpie swooped toward the house in triumph, perched for mere seconds on the porch rail in front of them all, and then followed its comrades into the barn. It seemed to bid the others to follow.

Before anyone could voice one of a hundred questions, Phoebe grabbed the door handle. "Now!" she whispered urgently, and stifling their whispered objections her five companions followed her in crouched trots out to the barn. Once inside they found that the stalls of three of Jim's horses had been unlatched. The magpies were working on three more. Phoebe made as if to open one of the gates.

"Hold on!" Dale exclaimed. "What in the world is going on?!"

"This is our only chance," Phoebe said, suddenly realizing she knew nothing about horses. Jim stepped in and took over, calming the horse and leading her out.

"Chance for what?" Dale said, "The whole world's gone crazy! First we were taking orders from a horse, now birds?"

"Listen," Phoebe implored adamantly, "all I know is that one of two animals is major-league BS-ing us right now, and my money says it's that horse! Stay if you want, but I'm getting out of here while I can!"

Dale was speechless. "Kind of a zoo, isn't it?" Chuck said with a grin.

"What about the bird that attacked Axl?" Antonia reasoned. Some of the others were wondering the same thing.

"I don't know!" Phoebe shouted. "I don't know what was wrong with that bird, I don't know what's wrong with these birds, and I don't know what's wrong with us. But we have a chance to get away from this terrible place and I'm taking it!"

"I am, too!" Axl agreed.

"Sign me up," Chuck added. Jim said nothing, but his haste to ready the horses made his intentions evident enough. Antonia and Dale were quickly converted by the prospect of staying behind to defend themselves.

Jim helped each of them mount, not trusting to chance that they would have time to saddle. Half of the group had never ridden before, so as Jim was mounting he whispered some quick pointers on how to ride. He knew riding bareback would be especially hard for the inexperienced group and he emphasized the absolute necessity to hold on and stay mounted. Once they all were mounted he wasn't sure what the next step was. But without any beckoning, all six horses suddenly advanced through the door, took stock of their surroundings, and then broke into a gallop straight toward the forest.

CHAPTER SIXTEEN
NINE GIANTS

The sun had just set when they escaped. The horses, guided by some unseen force, headed for a point in the trees that was at a far corner of the cleared portion of Jim's property: nearly a third of a mile away. They had advanced less than a hundred yards past the ranch house before the howling began and nine grotesque giants burst from their hiding places in pursuit.

The monsters were hideous and were covered in shaggy gray hair. The shortest of them was over seven feet tall and must have been at least five hundred pounds of Herculean might. Their hair was patchy in places, revealing leathery black skin that bulged with savage strength.

They were ape-like in shape, though they traveled exclusively on two legs in hunchback fashion. Their frames were wide (especially around their barrel chests) with lanky muscular arms nabbing and slashing while long muscular legs galloped forward with horrifying swiftness. Their ugly naked faces were fierce and simian, with just enough human in them to make the chase seem like villainy rather than guiltless instinct.

Black lips curled back to reveal mouths full of threatening yellow teeth, with long fang-like canines. Their yells were awful and deafening—something between a mule's howl and a sea lion's roar—followed by hoots and jabbers and trilling. As the company of strangers drew farther and farther from the light of the buildings the monsters became less and less distinct, the nine individual shapes morphing into one thrashing black mass. When the riders reached the edge of the trees only Old Jobe marked the monsters' advance, his white coat reflecting what little light there was in the dusk. Each of the riders hoped Jobe would turn around and fight. They'd seen some of his power when he'd threatened Phoebe and they knew he could have stopped the phalanx of sasquatches if he'd wanted to. But he did nothing. Phoebe had been right—Jobe ran ahead of the charging beasts like a captain, doing nothing to force them back. He was their leader.

All the while Jobe's eerie voice squealed at the escapees hoarsely in their minds: *"No! Stop! Come back!"*

All any of them could do was hold on for dear life to their horses, clutching tightly onto whatever ballast they trusted: arms around necks, fists full of mane, legs gripping torsos. The riding was rough and painful, the journey across the open field a perilous and frightening one. The horses were pushing the limits of their abilities though they had not been fed that day, and while this fact made Jim nervous, he knew that their speed was the only prayer of outrunning the giants.

Night was closing in and the winds whipped about the riders with a whistling to rival the howls of the Orliak. Then, just before they entered the forest, it started to rain. The rain led the fanfare of the storm by only a few minutes, then a cannonade of thunder and lightning began. For the next several hours all six of the strangers were blind travelers in the dark. The rain was so heavy, the trees so thick, the night so profoundly black that they could not fathom how all six horses could be travelling with such confidence, and without separating. More importantly, though, none could believe that the Orliak could possibly follow them under these conditions, and they were right.

They knew they were safe when, after nearly an hour of climbing and descending with prodigious swiftness, the horses slowed their pace considerably. Still they pressed on with deliberation, still they stayed in a consistent file, yet their urgency had diminished enough to allow for a reprieve. They did this for hours on end, all night in fact. Their course was not straight, and only Jim really noticed. He theorized that this was to make them harder to follow. How could horses be so clever? He never voiced any of these thoughts, though. Nobody spoke for the whole night save only three times: first, when the horses had slowed down for about fifteen minutes, Jim said, "I think we're safe now." This was intended to calm everybody's nerves and it worked. Second, an unexpected comment from Dale: "I actually kind of like the rain. I always have." Third, somewhere in the middle of the night, when Axl randomly said, "Phoebe, I think you were right."

Other than that, nobody spoke. Nobody slept. They dared not drift into the state of vulnerability that comes with sleep. All night they stayed awake, though blind in the darkness and nearly deaf in the storm. The wind and the rain made their clutched fists numb, but still they clutched. It made their clothes heavy and wet and sticky, but none regretted escaping Atlas Ranch, even with the future as uncertain as it was.

There would have been no way to know what time it was if not for Dale's watch and Antonia's phone. She was the only one who'd had her phone with her when they escaped. The rain started letting up after 1 a.m. and it had totally stopped by 2:30. To say that the sun came up that morning would have been an extreme exercise in faith, but it eventually became light enough to see, though the sky was still gray with clouds. Their journey had led them deep into the forests. The riders were surrounded on every side by gigantic conifers of every variety growing in terrain so rocky, dry, and uneven that it almost seemed impossible. The ground was a carpet of pinecones, pine needles, and other forest debris, with other plant life appearing only in tufts. Every bush was shapeless and overgrown, every stump and log was inhabited. There were no signs of man anywhere: no roads or houses or axes. It was a truly remote and unknown place, a sight which brought equal comforts as it did apprehensions.

With sight, speech also seemed to return. They all spoke in whispers and only one at a time, but each seemed confident that their sound wouldn't attract any unwanted attention. Jim did most of the talking for the first little while, just rattling off minutia about things they were seeing to take everybody's minds off of their peril. He talked about all the plants, the rocks, and the wildlife of the area. He talked about the history of Mackenzie, his life there, and the annual wildfires that were due any time now. He quickly decided that right then wasn't the best time to bring up that topic.

"Where do you think these horses are taking us?" Phoebe asked.

"I couldn't say," Jim answered. "These woods go on forever and I don't know how I'd begin to get my bearings, not with how much wandering around we did during the night."

His words didn't inspire much hope in the group beyond the inexplicable trust they felt in the horses. "How much of what Jobe said do you think is true?" Antonia asked to nobody in particular.

"None of it," Phoebe replied without hesitation.

"Well at least some of it," Chuck reasoned. "Those monsters were really there, that's for sure, and they definitely wanted to hurt us."

"So did Jobe," Phoebe added.

"Well yeah," Antonia conceded, "but all that stuff about Stynaksz and people coming to help us?"

"Maybe Jobe was Stynaksz," Axl theorized. "I didn't mention it, but when Dale and I asked him who he was the first time he just said, 'Jobe will suffice.' Who knows who he really was?"

"Does anybody else feel like this whole thing has now officially surpassed rational explanation?" Phoebe asked. All assented.

At 6 a.m., the group reached a point from which they could see a scattered cluster of houses. It was a town, for all intents and purposes, though it seemed to have been invaded by the wilderness and was mostly a collection of abandoned farms.

"What's that?" Axl asked hopefully to his uncle. "Do you know that place?"

Jim squinted, as usual. "That's Minersville, where Eric Lopez lives. If that's where the horses are taking us, they sure took a roundabout way of getting here. It's only about 15 miles from the ranch."

The horses didn't stop for Jim's considerations. He went straight into a history of the town, though. Hearing Jim talking so freely put everyone at ease. He'd retained enough facts to keep them entertained during their entire descent, which lasted for over an hour. Shoshone Indians had originally lived in the area in relative isolation due to the remoteness of the location. By the time that settlers started mining the area in the late 1800s the local tribe's numbers had decreased so much that they didn't put up any fight—in fact, they welcomed their new neighbors. Most of the Native Americans ended up moving down to the Fort Hall reservation and Eric was descended from one of the very few families that stayed around.

Minersville, of course, got its name from the hundreds of miners it attracted, who reaped a bounteous gold harvest from placer mining. The town had been booming with commerce for years. Restaurants, saloons, hotels, general stores—there'd even been talks of extending an arm of the railroad up there. Eric's ancestors integrated fully with the newcomers during this period and joined in the prosperity. Then the mines ran out. Now, with less than a hundred people living there, Minersville was considered a genuine old-west ghost town.

At the close of Jim's oration Chuck added, "And all those miners established the first 24-hour eatery in Boise County. That's part of the story right?"

"You could not possibly be hungry right now!" Phoebe laughed. "You only ate your weight in trail mix yesterday!"

"So did you!" Antonia interjected.

"No," Phoebe corrected, "technically I ate *your* weight in trail mix."

It was at that moment that the horses slowed to only a few plodding steps, then finally stopped in front of a little farm house at the edge of town. All of the houses seemed to be "at the edge of town." Out in front there was a familiar pickup truck and horse trailer, this time accompanied by a van. All three were stuffed with belongings—suitcases, brimmed-over cardboard boxes, and indelicately-packed furniture. It had all the signs of a move-out.

"This is Eric's house," Jim said. Many of the others had already guessed that.

"What are we doing here?" Dale asked.

They all sat, unsure of what to do, for several minutes. Suddenly a dark boy who could only have been Eric's son appeared through the front door carrying an over-stuffed backpack to the pickup. He stopped stunned when he saw the six ragged-looking bareback riders. They could not have appeared more tired, wet, and dirty if they'd just come from digging graves all night.

"Morning, son," Jim said, again forgetting that he was Axl. "Is your Dad around?"

As if on cue, Eric Lopez appeared in the doorway with his wife and daughter behind him. He took a few steps out, the oddest expression on his face. He didn't seem surprised, that's what was so odd about it. It was a steely gaze full of knowing, as if he'd expected to see them there all along. It was very unsettling.

"Morning, Jim," Eric greeted, looking straight at Axl. Jim was sure he was mistaken at Eric's apparent recognition and he made deliberate eye contact with his nephew to prompt him.

"Morning, Eric," Axl replied. "Today's the day, huh?"

Eric didn't respond, still seeming consumed by the thought behind his knowing gaze. He cocked his head a little to one side and asked emptily to the group, "What happened to *you*?"

They all smiled a little bit at the question and Chuck let out an audible laugh. "You wouldn't believe us if we told you," he answered.

Eric smiled a little and nodded. "Don't count on it," he said. He turned to his wife and whispered, "Would you take the kids down to the general store for a candy bar or something?"

"It's only 7 a.m.," she protested. "The general store isn't open yet."

"Then go down there and wait until it opens."

"In the truck?"

"No, walk," Eric said decisively. "I need some time alone."

Jim was generally the hardest member of the company to surprise. But even he was blown away not only by Eric Lopez's receptiveness to their story, but that Eric had anticipated it. He'd simply nodded through Jim's careful explanation of their situation. Eric did seem surprised at Jobe's role in the story, but otherwise he accepted each new development without contest.

"Come inside," Eric said at the end of Jim's narrative, "I have something I want to show you."

He disappeared back through the open door and all six riders, without even a thought for whether or not their horses would run away, dismounted and followed him. They had no bridles to tie up, not that there was anything to tie them to. Eric's fence had all but fallen down.

The house and land was in complete disrepair, as Eric had said. It was not as bad as Leroy Hobbes' place, but it was also a lot smaller and humbler. It at least had the feeling of a home, a quality afforded by the family that lived there which made it seem infinitely more welcoming. Still, the thistles and crabgrass that obscured the walkway were not persuading any of them to buy the house off Eric.

"My father's side is all Shoshone," Eric told them as he unpacked and repacked boxes in search of something, "My ancestors were what they called the 'Minersville Recluse' Indians because they were isolated from all the other tribes. Yep, this house is right in the place of the original homestead."

"Hold on," Phoebe said, "what are you talking about?"

All of the furniture had been packed so Eric sat cross-legged on the floor with the box as he rifled through it. One by one the others followed his example and sat on the floor. He finally pulled a roll of fabric out of the box and, spreading it out on the floor, said, "This. This is what I'm talking about."

They all gathered around it. It was a blanket or shawl of some kind and looked like it belonged in a museum. It was worn, faded, and frayed beyond repair at the edges. Very few of the original figures could be made out, their simple depictions having lost first their details and then their color. For most of them all that remained were faint outlines or shapes—trees were merely triangles.

The design in the center was the best-preserved, though it had also undergone apparent aging. The artwork was crude, but even had it been more literal they might not have been able to interpret the strange scene. A small crowd of Indian boys gathered in apparent reverence to a tall eyeless figure with a head shaped like a diamond. Next to the figure was a towering triangular shape that defied explanation. It was clearly not a tree and seemed too big to represent a tent. Was it a mountain?

"What are we looking at?" asked Dale.

"My grandmother used to tell me a story about this blanket," Eric told them. "She said it was an old story and probably not true—she was always careful to say 'probably.' That always kept me wondering." As he spoke he pointed to different symbols with his wrinkled brown hands. "She said that this is our forest, and this scene is somewhere near Minersville. There used to be a jagged line at the top to show the mountains but it's too frayed to see now.

"The Shoshone have lived in Idaho for a long time. My ancestors lived in this area since long before the whites showed up and we remained here even after they'd settled. My ancestors were too important to the treasure hunters to be forced out. We built this homestead as part of our integration.

"But this scene is from long before that. Grandma said this blanket told about an old secret that the Recluse Shoshone kept. She said that long ago an angel came down to teach the young hunters. She said some people called it a spirit or a monster or a shaman, but she always called it an angel in her story.

"The angel was very proud of the Recluse Shoshone and admired their skills in hunting and battle. He said that he was going to make them superior over all beasts and men. All he asked for was young braves to teach. He took them up to the mountain and he taught them how to inhabit the bodies of the beasts. They used the wolves' speed to hunt their food, the bear's strength to fell tall trees, and the hawk's stealth to spy on their enemies.

"The angel left them, but they remembered what he taught. For generations they passed on the knowledge and kept it a secret from everyone, even from their allies. The angel had warned them to tell no one and promised to punish them if they broke his trust. He said he would always be watching them. Grandma said the angel could even hear their thoughts.

"Because of this, they couldn't hide it from him when a stupid young brave had offered to teach one of the whites in a barter agreement. The angel stayed true to his word. He sent monsters to kill everyone who had learned his magic. Most of the tribe died, others fled to southern tribes. Only a few families remained. My ancestors were among them."

"What sorts of monsters?" Axl asked as soon as the story finished.

"That I don't know," Eric answered. "Grandmother said that there was a companion blanket to this one that showed the consequences of disobeying the angel, but it's been lost and I've never seen it."

"I'm confused," Antonia said. "That story made you believe us? About our souls switching and everything?"

"It was a couple of things, actually," Eric explained. "Several years ago when I was visiting relatives in Fort Hall I met an old man who everyone called crazy, and they were right. He said that he'd been living for hundreds of years and that he'd stayed alive by claiming a new body whenever he got too old. It was kind of funny, too, because there were a bunch of different names he'd respond to. It reminded me of Grandma's story a little, except her story was cool and his was creepy. But I've thought about what he said a lot since then, and how Grandma's story was just 'probably not true.'

"But the other day when I came to Atlas Ranch, and Axl talked so much like Jim and Jim didn't seem to know how to be himself, that reminded me again. And when I met Antonia LeBlanc, who didn't correct me when I said I saw her fight Rita Squires in Las Vegas…"

"That's right," Antonia interrupted, "it was Marian Murphy in Vegas. Rita Squires was in Atlantic City. I *did* pick up on that but didn't say anything."

Eric nodded and then turned to Axl. "It was too absurd to ask you, Jim, but if you had so much as suggested it to me I would have believed it. I know you're not the sort to joke around like this."

"I appreciate your trust, Eric," Jim said, "and your story. I just wish we knew what it all meant."

"Hopefully it means we're that much closer to finding that angel," Chuck said. "He seems to be the guy to talk to when you've got a soul-transfer problem."

Jim examined the blanket again. "You don't happen to know what mountain this is, do you?" he asked, pointing to the enormous pyramid in the middle.

"No, I don't," Eric admitted, "and I'm not totally sure that it is a mountain. Grandma said she didn't know what it was."

Jim nodded slightly, suddenly noticing something else that had been in the same box with the blanket. It was a small metal triangle with a thin leather band laced through a hole in the middle to form a necklace. It was almost identical to the one on his keychain.

There was a faint tapping at the door. Axl gasped audibly. He was justifiably jumpy. Eric looked confusedly at the faces of the others as if they knew who his guest would be. He arose with a tired groan, then went and opened the door. At his feet a magpie stood alertly.

"Right on time," Chuck murmured.

CHAPTER SEVENTEEN

THE OBELISK

The horses took them as far as they could. They traveled for hours into the woods with only the magpie as their guide. The horses seemed to know where they were going, but still the magpie was always leading the way, flying a little and perching a little. Eric had given them directions to a restaurant in town where they could eat breakfast but they didn't want to waste any time. They shared a few cans of Vienna sausages that Eric hadn't packed. Lunchtime came and went and nobody mentioned it. All were sore and stiff from their last long ride but nobody complained. All could sense that the end of their troubles was close at hand.

Whereas their course from the night before had meandered left, right, up, and down, this one seemed only to gain in altitude. What's more, their path seemed to be becoming increasingly rugged. As the hike became more treacherous, as they became wearier, and as the air became colder, they knew they wouldn't want to spare breath for talking so they talked while they could.

"Do you think Brodie will be alright?" Axl asked his uncle.

"Yeah, I do," Uncle Jim answered. "I got up early yesterday before breakfast and set him up in the shed with food and water. It's not the best place on the property, but it's comfortable and it'll keep him safe and out of trouble."

"Hey, Dale," Chuck asked off-handedly, "what is this thing you have against dogs?"

"I'd rather not say." Dale answered, "Maybe another time." Chuck dropped it. "What about you?" Dale asked in return, "Do you think your wife will be okay?"

"I know she will be," Chuck said, "I mean, of course she's worried sick and she's miserable on her own, but Jules can take care of herself. Just the same, if one of you suddenly comes up with some way to fix our problem, I'd love to know about it."

"I think we're all about to know," Antonia said. The horses had stopped walking.

At the foot of a steep and rocky peak the horses knelt, bidding their riders to dismount. Their path would be a narrow one and the horses could not continue.

The magpie continued to lead them, keeping high overhead but well within view. The sky was still gray but the day was warm, for which all six were grateful. They'd had no way to change their wet clothes, which had just begun to dry. They climbed on with steady pace, regardless of their conditions. It was not an easy climb. Much of it was so steep that it took them to their knees and the rocks and gravel beneath their feet made them slide and scrape their legs and arms. Breathing became more and more of a labor and their sweat felt colder and colder as they climbed higher and met with wind.

The difficulty of the climb made it seem to last for days. Hours passed with nothing to see but more rocks and trees, though the trees were sparser up here. Time after time they thought they were almost to the top but were met with only more mountain. They never reached the top.

The veiled sun was only a few hours away from setting when their magpie began to screech excitedly, dancing around on its perch. The six of them stood staring on in confusion, trying to discern what the strange and unexpected object was that it stood on.

The object stuck several feet out of the ground and looked like a shard of a giant looking-glass. Irregular in its shape and dimensions, the object tapered to a point on its upper end where the magpie stood. It was thick and heavy-looking, and strangest of all it shone back with a distorted reflection of its surroundings due to its original conical construction. Its mirrored surface was smudged and chipped by the elements, but the six strangers could see their reflections clearly enough.

What was it? Some sort of monument? An obelisk? A pyramid? The bird squawked over their questions, still hopping and flapping on the tip of the cone. It seemed almost frustrated. Finally it hopped off its perch and onto the stones obscuring the base of the cone and continued its expressive dance there. Jim thought he understood. He approached and began rolling the stones away. The bird stopped squawking.

They found that the cone was only submerged in the rocks a few feet; it was evidently the broken-off tip of something else. Almost immediately Axl noticed the glint of something similar twenty yards away. The group went to the spot and began digging. This excavation took several hours and only revealed the uppermost portion of a massive triangular hull covered in the chromium-like mirrored plating. Dale didn't help rolling away the stones, not immediately. He was measuring the perceivable length of the object with his feet. The exposed portion alone must have been forty feet long. They would never discover the full amazing scale of the object.

"What is it?" Dale asked.

"I don't know," Jim answered, "some sort of aircraft."

There was a silence full of wonder, dread, and excitement. Phoebe ended it. "Okay, fine," she finally said, "we're all thinking it: this is a spaceship." There was a silence of concurrence.

There was a void in the ship's shell where the tip had been torn away. It faced them tauntingly, its interior black with shadow. The six stood staring into its depths confoundedly. The magpie suddenly reappeared, perching for a moment at the uppermost rim of the jagged ring that formed the entrance. It looked at them. Its beady black eyes were so inexpressive. What did the look mean? Was it bidding them to enter? Warning them to stay back? Had they completed what it had brought them here to do? Then all at once the bird was gone, dropping into a glide and disappearing into the depths of the injured derelict vessel.

Nobody was sure what to do. Axl fidgeted. So did Dale. "Does he want us to follow him?" Dale asked.

"I don't know," was all Jim said. He was, by nature, a man of action. His long life had proved that over and over again. But for now he was being uncharacteristically reserved.

The six of them stood frozen with trepidation. What wonders would they find in this interstellar ruin? What horrors? Were any of them worthy of the great knowledge hidden within? Who were they to decide whether that knowledge was to be shared or concealed or destroyed? They were standing on the precipice that so many others had stood on in such moments since the dawn of man: moments of invention or discovery, when the fire of gods was within reach, and one had only to decide if they were Prometheus enough to take it.

Nobody moved for almost five minutes. Then Phoebe collapsed, thrashing. She squealed and growled and seemed oblivious to the harsh rocks beneath her as she writhed. The others made as if to go to her, but not one of them could reach her before meeting the same fate. So dizzying and turbulent was the sensation that it never entered into any of their minds that they'd felt the exact same thing for the first time only days before. It was the upheaval they'd been waiting for.

The sky was clear that night. The moon shone especially bright on the mountaintop where the spaceship lay mostly buried, where the trees were so thin that they left the summit nearly bald. It was not a place that received many visitors. The way was treacherous and there was no trail, and the reward was a view inferior to that from any other neighboring mountain. But had any traveler happened to be hiking in the neighborhood that night, they could not have dismissed an eerily out-of-place chorus of cheers and laughter, for the echoing fanfare retreated and returned in ecstatic bursts for over an hour.

Each of the six—no longer strangers—had been restored to their proper frames.

All were only too excited to return home and take their lives back up again. Even Phoebe had decided that it was time to return home. Axl couldn't stop running his fingers through the smooth dark locks he'd missed calling his own, especially after seeing how good they looked from unfamiliar perspectives. He even ran his tongue along his braces with a hint of nostalgia. Being a cowboy would be nice, being famous would be nice, but all of sudden it felt so good just to be Axl.

Chuck was clearly happy to be back in his own body, scratching his bristly beard and slapping his paunch with satisfaction. It goes without saying, of course, that Antonia had missed her body most of all, though she did feel some very obvious effects of neglect. Still, she didn't let that spoil her celebration of the reunion.

Notwithstanding the deepening darkness of night, the descent was faster than the climb. Nobody could tell how close they were to getting back to the bottom, partly because the whole scene looked entirely different in the dark and partly because their winged guide would disappear and reappear unexpectedly. They hadn't seen the bird in a good twenty minutes. They all imagined they were making very good time—Chuck had even invited them to come to church with him until he realized that Sunday was over and the next workweek had nearly started.

Still, all were very surprised when the first horse came back into view. It was Fiona, the white one. No. No it wasn't. It was her shade, a sort of ghastly wretched twin sent in her place. They hadn't arrived back at their horses at all. It was Old Jobe waiting for them. They stopped dead. The horse stood panting, looking more spent than ever after its long climb.

"I told you not to leave," came the telepathic voice.

"Yeah, we know," Phoebe announced in her own youthful voice with her own mocking tone, "because you wanted to keep us safe, right? From the giants?"

"You could have stopped them and you didn't," Antonia shouted at him. "You lied to us!"

"You fools! You don't understand!" Jobe defended himself angrily, stamping his hoof. *"You have no idea what you've bumbled into."*

"And we want nothing to do with it!" Dale cut in. Phoebe sounded an assent, followed by Jim, Antonia, Chuck, and Axl in unison.

"Stynaksz will not spare Earth. Your planet's obscurity is the only virtue that preserves it. Once he has chopped down the mightier trees he will pluck up the seedlings."

"Listen, unless you're offering to give me a ride home, I've got nothing to say to you," Chuck jeered with surprising levity.

"We are worthless to you now," came Axl's final provocative call.

"What's that?" answered the cerebral voice. *"What are you talking about?"*

Axl spoke, the others nodded. "We're back to normal, all of us. We found your ship up in the mountains. It changed us back."

"My...ship?" came the voice, coarse with ghastly surprise. He was silent for a long moment. *"Your condition has been rectified, then?"*

"Yes," Axl answered.

The horse continued to stare, its eyes still full of knowing but still devoid of emotion, even as the words came: *"Then you are of no more use to me."* Jobe paused a moment more, then turned and galloped away.

"What did he mean by that?" Dale asked, unsettled.

"He meant we'd better go find those horses!" Jim urged, grabbing his companion's shoulders and arms and pushing them along.

Somewhere in the distance there was an otherworldly howl. Then there was another. The giants were getting closer.

CHAPTER EIGHTEEN

KATABASIS

This time the Orliaks would take them. They had no horses and very little strength left. As quickly as it had come, their celebrating had vanished and dread had taken its place.

All the terrors of the last three days culminated in an hour of pitch-black flight, the light of the moon blotted out by a canopy of trees. There was no way of knowing if the thudding in their ears was heartbeats or footfalls, no way of knowing if the panting was that of man or beast, no way of knowing if the snapping of branches and twigs was from their own feet or from that of the giants. The only person to say anything was Dale who, in his frenzy of fright and exhaustion, muttered without ceasing in his sobbing tones, "We're gonna die, we're gonna die!"

It was only by providence that they were able to make it so far without more than stumbles to slow them down. With such complete blindness, it seemed they could hardly have gone a hundred yards without one of them incurring a serious injury. It was Phoebe who finally did.

In the darkness she slipped on a wet patch of moss. It was a dizzying disorientation not unlike she'd experienced during their corporeal transference: slipping, tripping, falling, rolling, flailing, and then pain, an intense stabbing pain in her twisted ankle. She let out a shriek.

There had been six separate pairs of footfalls. Three continued, so spread out that they hadn't heard Phoebe's call. Jim and Antonia had stopped. "Phoebe!" Antonia called into the blackness. A strained groan came in reply.

"Sound off!" Jim called. "Help us find you!"

She grunted again, clutching blindly at her ankle. "I'm here!" she screamed through the pain.

Antonia knew she was closest by the sounds of the two voices. "Again!" Antonia called.

"Here!" Phoebe cried.

Antonia felt her way toward the voice in half a crouch, feeling along the ground with one hand and along the trees with the other.

"Again!"

"Here!"

Antonia was almost to Phoebe when another sound joined them: heavy galloping footfalls. Not of horses, not of men. Monsters.

"Again!" Antonia screamed again frantically, almost angrily.

Phoebe hesitated. "No!" she called, "Go on, run! Don't ask me if I'm serious, I am!" Phoebe felt Antonia's groping hands fall across her face. "They might stop chasing if they have me…" Phoebe began to reason.

"Get up," Antonia said, finding Phoebe's narrow shoulders and grasping them soundly.

"Antonia, I think my ankle is broken, just let them…"

Antonia repeated herself with more severity: "Get. Up." Phoebe moved her leg. She winced at the pain of her dragging ankle and sobbed audibly.

"Where are you?" Jim's voice came again. He hadn't abandoned them.

"Right behind you!" Antonia called, "Go! Go! Go!" Without another word she felt around for her desired grips and hoisted Phoebe into her arms, running in the direction Jim's voice had come from. She was not a moment too soon.

The Orliaks were not as blind in the dark as the humans and they were much faster—especially than Antonia burdened with Phoebe. Phoebe had resigned herself to the death that inevitably awaited. She felt she deserved it. She hadn't lived a good life, she'd run away from home, and now her parents would never even know what had happened to their daughter. She'd had so little going for her, she thought. Now Antonia, who had everything going for her, was going to die too. She begged to be sacrificed to the sasquatches.

"Shut up!" Antonia responded breathlessly. She'd set her course toward a broad beam of moonlight amidst the trees. As they neared, it grew larger and clearer: it was a clearing. The others had paused there to wait for them to catch up, but as soon as Dale heard one of the monsters bellow he turned and kept running.

Jim appeared out of the trees and shouted after him: "The gun, Dale! You have a gun! Use your gun!"

Dale stopped and started fumbling in his pocket for the .357 Magnum revolver. So did Axl.

"I don't know how to use a gun!" Dale shouted in dismay.

"Well, figure it out!" Jim shouted back.

Antonia was mere strides away from the clearing but knew the monsters would overtake her before she got there. She dropped Phoebe indelicately, turned, and found herself with just enough light and just enough time to set up for the attack.

The monster bounded as if to pounce on the fighter. She took position and put all of her strength into a roundhouse that caught the monster squarely in the ribs. It squealed and stumbled off target. While it recovered its footing Antonia set up for another attack but was relieved to see the other monsters rush right past her toward the clearing.

Dale had never so much as touched a revolver before. He was all but paralyzed from his fright but managed to hold the gun out in front of him and pull the trigger. Nothing happened.

"Take the safety off!"

"The what?"

Jim was running toward him with all his might. Meanwhile Axl had gathered himself and was taking aim at the monster closest to his uncle. Jim had been right: it was nothing like shooting bottles lined up on a fence. Jim had also said that even the best gunmen could miss by a hair on their first shot. If Axl missed by a hair it could mean his uncle's life.

He held it with both hands, partly to straighten his aim and party to keep the gun from shaking. He was so scared he was on the verge of tears. He pulled the trigger. The report rang out in the mountains and the monster howled as the shot, intended for his shoulder, hit him in the neck. It was providence alone that had guided the shot and Axl knew it.

There was such a flurry of shadows and sounds that, even after the event, nobody could say for sure just how many creatures there were. At least four, maybe eight. Axl killed the one that had nearly overtaken Jim, giving his uncle just enough time to reach Dale, grab the gun, and turn to respond to another creature closing the twenty-five feet between them. He shot the monster square in the chest.

Chuck was not equipped to fight the monster that finally overtook him, but he did what came naturally. The monster was so close that Chuck could feel drops of its vile drool shower the back of his neck when it roared at him. He dropped to the ground and rolled as if trying to put out a fire in his clothes, then turned on his back and brought his legs up to defend himself. He kicked blindly and furiously as the beast nabbed at him. Chuck's blows were only sufficient to deflect the monster's first few advances. Finally the creature grabbed Chuck by the ankle with one iron-gripped hand and then grabbed him by the neck with the other. With prodigious strength the giant raised Chuck over its head as if ready to tear him apart. Axl fired three more hasty shots, aiming lower for fear of hitting Chuck. One bullet merely grazed the monster's knee, the next hit the monster in the left side of its gut, and the final one pierced into its heart. When the monster dropped the cook he did hurt Chuck's neck and wrists, but at least the massive grotesque body fell clear of him.

When Antonia found herself and Phoebe alone with the first monster she advanced on him. She'd always been a better offensive fighter than a defensive. She knew that in such an imbalanced match most of her techniques would be worthless. The monster was feet—not inches—taller than she was and weighed several hundreds of pounds more. She worried that she had hurt her leg with her first blow but she knew she had to keep fighting.

The monster hadn't fully regained its wits or its footing when Antonia attacked. There was barely enough light to see what she was doing but she acted quickly and kept on her guard. The beast's head and torso were too high off the ground for a practical attack so Antonia focused on its lower half, striking the monster over and over again with her knees and elbows. She felt that her first blow to the monster's ribs had been the best placed, so whenever possible she went back to that spot, elbowing it or punching it or kicking it.

The giant had no particular technique, only tremendous brute strength and a savage instinct to fight and kill. Antonia knew if she let the monster get a grip she had no prayer of breaking it, so anytime one of the gargantuan hands came near her she focused on deflecting or escaping it. The match seemed to last for ages but Antonia knew it was probably less than a minute or two. She couldn't have lasted much longer. She hadn't eaten in almost a day and had been travelling almost nonstop for longer. All she had left to burn was adrenaline, but even on her best day she would've been no match for this creature in any ring.

She didn't know who fired the first few shots but it was clear that the marksman could see no more than a blurry silhouette of combat in the trees. A bullet whizzed past Antonia's ear. "Watch it!" she screamed, "You're gonna kill me!"

She was conscious that Phoebe was probably still lying somewhere on the forest floor. She prayed that retreating into the clearing wouldn't bring the beast to Phoebe, but she knew her only chance was bringing the giant within range of the guns. She created some distance between her and the monster and then sprinted away. It followed her with rage in its step. Antonia's heart had never beaten harder, never from joy, never from excitement, never from fear.

In her life she'd experienced so much of pleasure and so much of dread, but she always knew them to be temporary. This was the first time that death seemed real to her, that within seconds her lifetime of training and conditioning could fail her. The giant's natural gifts of size and might would trump years' worth of time spent in gyms and studios and dojos. If virtue didn't exist and all that mattered in the world was strength—if the most powerful creatures in the world deserved to have what they wanted simply because they had the power to seize it—then there would have been no tragedy in Antonia LeBlanc's death. Victory would have belonged to a deserving victor.

She was mere strides ahead of her pursuer when she came into the light and all of a sudden perceived Jim rushing in her direction. She'd have to trust that his aim would be true from fifty yards away. She did a flying baseball dive into the tall grasses, curled into a ball, and cried a prayer of five frantic words: "God, please make it stop!"

Jim fired twice. Both shots hit the monster in the head. It stumbled backwards and collapsed five feet from Antonia.

Whatever the number of monsters had truly been at the beginning, after four had been killed the attack was over and there were no more giants to be seen. In the course of the attack Axl had used up all shots in his revolver and Jim had used half of his. They were all grateful to be alive notwithstanding their injuries. All would heal, though Jim silently worried what all this trauma would do to Axl later in life. Or Dale. Or any of them, really. Despite his bravery, Antonia's bravery, Phoebe's—all of them had revealed to the others and themselves what their dispositions were in the face of true terror.

Antonia was the strongest of them notwithstanding her fatigue and she would have been prepared to carry the injured girl the rest of the way if she'd had to. But just as she was helping her limping comrade into the light of the moon, six horses entered the clearing.

CHAPTER NINETEEN
ABDUCTION

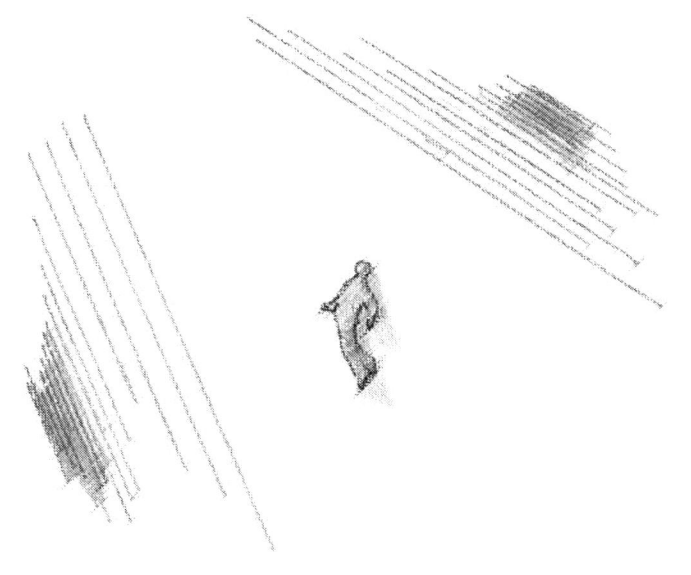

The horses did not rush back to the ranch; they seemed almost conscious of the infirmities of their riders and rode at a pace for their comfort. Antonia was relieved that this bizarre four-day episode was almost over and had returned to stressing about her obligations to her agent and director. Still, she was sensitive to the delicate conditions of the others, some of whom were in no shape for a speedy bareback journey.

It was about 4 a.m. Monday morning when they got back to the ranch. Many were eager for speedy departures so they said their goodbyes and voiced their plans for the immediate future during the journey. Jim would give Dale, Chuck, and Axl time to gather their things, and then he'd drive the two men home on his way to the airport. They could make Axl's pre-scheduled flight back to Seattle if they hurried. By now Phoebe was eager to return to her home in Oregon as soon as possible and Jim offered to buy her a ticket and drop her off at the airport with Axl. Antonia insisted on buying the ticket to thank Jim for his kindness and hospitality.

Phoebe thanked Antonia and then said, mostly in jest, "Is that going to come out of the $4,000 you owe me?"

"No," Antonia laughed, "I'll write you a check."

The ranch came back in view then. The horses hadn't taken them back through Minersville this time so the company hadn't seen a house all day. It was a welcome sight for Jim and, to a lesser extent, Axl, but for the others the feeling of dread about the place would never truly go away. How could they explain this to anyone? How could they explain it to themselves? Strange supernatural animals, telepathic voices, derelict spaceships, and transferred souls? How much of what Jobe had told them was true? Was there really a war going on somewhere in the stars? Was there really an enemy somewhere named Stynaksz?

They dismounted the horses in front of the barn. Jim went in to close their stalls. Axl followed.

"Here's your hat back, Uncle Jim," Axl said, offering the cowboy hat to his uncle.

"Keep it," Jim smiled as he worked, "you look good in it."

"Really? I can keep it?"

"Sure. Axl, I was proud of you these few days—"

Phoebe's voice interrupted as she called his name from the porch: "Jiiiim!"

The five others kept a cautious distance from the porch as they waited for Jim. He was just as amazed and confused by what he saw as they were. There, curled up protectively on the porch, wedged between a bench and the wall, was Leroy Hobbes. His breaths came laboriously and he barely blinked, his circular eyes glistening.

"Leroy?" Jim said, mounting the first step and placing his hands on his hips, laying a finger on the grip of his revolver unconsciously. "What's up, Leroy?"

At first Mr. Hobbes only muttered to himself unintelligibly. Jim repeated his question. Finally, the face that looked perpetually startled turned to Jim and said, "Heya, Pal."

That voice—not the voice but the inflection, the accent. "Pal"—Leroy Hobbes never called anyone "Pal." All at once Jim knew it and so did Chuck.

"Beaker?" Chuck asked, stepping forward.

Nobody argued. Axl never mentioned his impending flight, Antonia never mentioned her pressing engagement, Chuck never mentioned his sick-with-worry wife. Jim invited Stanley inside and sat him down on the couch. All of them gathered around. They had imagined their interview with the boy going differently. It didn't look like Stanley, but it was clear what had happened: the boy was now in his father's body.

Jim whispered to each of them not to frighten the boy. They wanted him to feel comfortable and ready to talk. In similarly hushed tones he asked Chuck, one of Stanley's closest friends, to conduct the interview.

Chuck put himself right in front of Stanley, sitting on one of the ottomans. Stanley was quieter now and sat more still, but his throat still vibrated as if he was muttering inside his mouth. He didn't make eye contact for the whole of the interview.

"Stanley," Chuck said, "what happened? How did you get like this?"

Stanley was silent for a moment, his eyes still studying the rocks in the fireplace. Finally he began. "Hey, Chuck, do you remember when I turned twenty-six?"

"Yeah," Chuck said, confused by the question, "That was last year. You came to the restaurant and we made you a cake with a '26' on it. Everybody sang 'Happy Birthday' to you."

Stanley nodded a lot, still not making eye contact. "My dad got me a flashlight because my old one broke. I tried it out in the woods that night and I walked a long, long way, really far away from my house. It took a long, long time and I got super lost."

Stanley remained silent for a long time after that. Chuck looked back to Jim with a questioning look. Jim raised his eyebrows and nodded. "What happened then, Stanley?"

"Somebody started talking to me. A man. I was scared because I was way out in the woods so I thought it was a killer, but then I couldn't see anyone so I thought it was a spook. But you know what, Chuck?"

The boy waited for Chuck to respond. It was a long wait. "What?" Chuck finally replied.

"It wasn't a killer or a spook. It was an alien."

Chuck heard somebody behind him swallow hard. Outside the sky had darkened with clouds and the wind had picked up. The horrors of Saturday night's escape were all coming back. Without Phoebe realizing it, tears had started to form in her eyes.

"What did he look like?" Chuck asked.

"I couldn't see him, he was in my head," Stanley said. "But he said that I shouldn't be afraid because he just wanted to help me. He said he was going to take me to his spaceship and help me quit smoking."

A few in the group made awkward sounds. They were the sounds that came out when nervous tension had built up and met with confusion. What was he talking about?

"He wanted to help you quit smoking?" Chuck asked almost skeptically.

"Yup," Stanley nodded again. "And he did, too! Didn't you notice, Chuck?"

"Oh, yeah," Chuck said, then asked, "but how did he help you quit?"

Stanley got excited, stuttering a little as he explained: "H-he showed me how to put my body inside a cat b-body…"

"Your body?"

"Not my real one. My astral body, that's what the alien called it. He said that my real body was addicted to nicotine and that the nicotine would keep me from quitting. He said that whenever I wanted nicotine I could trade bodies with my cat and I wouldn't want it so bad anymore. It worked great, too! One time…"

"Hold on, Beaker," Chuck interrupted. "How did you end up in your dad's body?"

Stanley's eyes dropped despondently from the fireplace to the floor. He was silent for a long time. "Beaker?" Chuck said again.

There was a sob in Stanley's voice. "He was mad at me..."

"Your dad?"

"No, the alien. He wanted to know how I messed all your bodies up at Hometown the other day. I told him I didn't know. He kept talking to me and wouldn't go away. He sounded mad. He said he was coming to get me and take me away. He said he was coming tonight." Stanley had an interrupting thought, then continued. "Sometimes when I want to smoke really bad I trade bodies with my dad when he's asleep. I thought if I did that tonight then the aliens wouldn't be able to find me. Sometimes they have a hard time finding me and they can't do anything, not even talk to me. I think they got my dad by mistake though, they got him..."

That was the point when Phoebe couldn't hold it in anymore. "How many aliens are there?" she blurted out.

"What do they look like, Stanley?" Dale added. Everybody voiced their questions at once.

"How do you change bodies?"

"How many times have you been to their spaceship?"

"What does the spaceship look like? Is it triangular? Does it have a shell like a mirror?"

"Did you change us up on purpose? How did it happen?"

Jim's first instinct was to quiet them all down and introduce the questions one by one but the curiosity was too controlling. Stanley still didn't make eye contact but his eyes were darting all around the room. The competing voices, the shouting, the interrogating tones—it was all so overwhelming. He felt on the verge of having another stress-induced seizure.

"Shut up!" he screamed suddenly. "Shut up!" he screamed again. All of them were silent. He looked at them now, making eye contact with each before finally focusing on Chuck. "Shut up!" he screamed again.

"Okay, Beak, okay," Chuck comforted.

"Shut up!" Stanley screamed again, casting accusingly at the others.

"We get it, Stanley, it's okay," Chuck said, "we've all stopped talking."

Stanley's eyes widened even wider and he asked with a trembling voice, "Then why do I still hear voices?" Suddenly there was a frantic scratching sound at the door. Brodie had broken out of the shed and was whimpering urgently, trying to get back inside. He barked and then retreated clumsily beneath the porch. Jim had never known Brodie to be a coward.

Stanley's eyes shot up to the ceiling and in one frantic motion he was on his feet. Stanley darted for the door. The others followed.

Bursting out into the dirt courtyard Stanley left his confounded pursuers on the porch. He flew, he stumbled, he recovered, all the way scratching violently at the back of his neck. Jim kept coming after him for a few steps then stopped. All of them saw it: descending slowly and materializing as it came, an enormous ship like the one they'd uncovered on the mountain. Its mirrored surface glinted back the lights from the house, their own reflections distorted in its angled surface. Brodie whined loudly.

All were stunned but Stanley. As soon as he realized the closeness of the ship he staggered and retreated toward the house. But he was too late. A blinding flash of light burst forth, bright enough and large enough to obscure every inch of the space pyramid. It kept going and going and going, white and cold light claiming every inch of visible space. The company on the porch took cover behind chairs and pillars and bannisters. Jim shielded his squinted eyes just enough to see the vague outline of Leroy Hobbes's body, writhing and flailing, being drawn through the air toward the focal point of the blast. Jim watched Stanley grow smaller and smaller as he ascended higher and higher until all Jim could see was oppressive brilliant light. Jim closed his eyes while he let out a yelp, covered his face, and dropped to his knees.

The light continued to blind them for only seconds more after that. It had gotten what it came for. By the time any of them dared open their eyes the ship had disappeared again.

CHAPTER TWENTY
SAYING GOODBYE

Jim didn't fully recover his sight for two days. He could see shapes and washed out colors within an hour of the abduction but everything else came back very gradually. Axl told his parents there'd been an accident and that he'd missed his flight. Uncle Jim had promised to send him home as soon as he could. Axl alone was willing to stay in Mackenzie any longer than he had to. Everyone else suggested that Jim abandon the house immediately and go somewhere else, but Jim was adamant. It was over. He was sure of it.

By the time the ship disappeared, Phoebe was beside herself. This last episode had pushed everyone a little beyond their limits, but Phoebe especially. The thrashing image of the man being helplessly drawn toward the ship—he almost looked like he was drowning. It was the image that had come to Phoebe in her nightmares for so many nights.

Antonia left her hysterical friend in the care of Dale while she went to pack all their belongings. Axl attended to Jim while Chuck called his wife. Julie would come to pick Chuck and Dale up at Atlas Ranch; Antonia's sports car wouldn't fit all of them and Jim was in no condition to drive his truck.

It occurred to Chuck while on the phone with Julie that the giants had built a crude barricade to block the driveway. In their absence someone—or, more likely, some*thing*—had moved it. They didn't question.

The farewells bid when each of them left were less endearing than the ones they'd shared on their way back from the mountain. They all seemed rushed, as if trying to escape before the next paranormal phenomenon took place. Antonia and Phoebe were the first to leave. Antonia abandoned all practicality and technique when packing, making a mess of her suitcase and leaving several things behind. She didn't care. She plugged her phone in just long enough to buy Phoebe a plane ticket, wrote a hasty $4,000 check and left it in Phoebe's backpack along with all of Phoebe's belongings as well as some of her own. She packed the small collection of bags into her Porsche, found Phoebe, and then gave Jim a quick hug around the neck. "Thanks for everything Jim, really. I hope you get better soon. Goodbye." She leaned in and put her mouth next to Axl's ear and whispered, "Do everything you can to talk Jim into leaving, ok? It's not safe here."

Phoebe was still too shaken up to say anything to Jim, but she also hugged him. Antonia and Phoebe were out of sight a minute later. Dale's farewell was no longer than Antonia's, and Chuck was so excited to be reunited with Julie that he almost forgot to say goodbye. He ran back up to the living room where Axl sat with Jim. "What do you think?" Chuck asked the boy, "Can you handle things around here? Can you take care of your uncle?"

"I think so," Axl said with a weak smile.

Chuck made another full turn, taking one last look at the house and the yard, and then said, "Jim, I really think you ought to come stay with me and Julie. Just for a little while. Just in case something else happens."

"It's over, Chuck," Jim said, wincing. "We both know it. You can feel it, can't you?"

Chuck was at a loss for words, but against his own rational reasoning he knew Jim was right. He nodded and sighed. "I'll come back tomorrow sometime to check on you. Thanks for everything, Jim. And you too, Axl."

Chuck did come back the next day. Jim was doing a lot better and had already bought Axl a plane ticket. That would be Chuck's last time on Atlas Ranch. For the rest of his time in Mackenzie he'd welcome opportunities to see his friend, just never on the ranch. The ranch held too much dread for the cook. He and Julie put their home and their restaurant up for sale within a month and moved down to Meridian, where Julie had family. They knew they could never tell their family about what had happened in those four days, and on several different occasions the six strangers had agreed not to tell anyone. Chuck and Julie were satisfied to get back to their simple, happy life and pretend the whole thing had never happened. Keeping the secret was a necessary part of their dream—more than a dream, a goal: to be normal people working normal jobs and living normal lives. They'd be people who knew nothing of alien secrets and telepathy. And when their daughter, Dayna, was born shortly after their move, she helped their dream seem more real.

Dale kept working as a barber but moved closer to his job. In truth, his new home was less than 30 miles away from his old one, but he'd lived in such a small, familiar world that 30 miles seemed like 300. It was perfect: he was still near enough to Mackenzie to honor his mother's memory and to run into Chuck and Jim but far enough away not to fear Old Jobe or alien spaceships. For all its unpleasantries, the experience had changed Dale for the better: to equal degrees Dale was now more appreciative of his simple life but now felt capable of little adventures outside his comfort zone. This development came not a moment too soon. The next year another person came into his life to fill the void left by his mother's death—a woman: Aurora Noel.

Aurora had been the thin woman he'd spoken to in Hometown Inn that fateful morning. She, too, had been caught in the astral displacement. For a fleeting moment Aurora and Stanley Hobbes had traded bodies, then back again, then forth again, then back again. She'd fled from fear and kept the experience a secret, sure that nobody would believe her. But her curiosity finally brought her back to the little town in search of the truth. It led her to Dale Merchant.

Phoebe returned to her parents and was reconciled quickly. Unlike the others, she broke her vow of silence almost immediately. None of them would have blamed her; Phoebe had been so deeply disturbed by the whole experience that she had to tell someone. Her parents were patient and sympathetic but were also certain that the whole demented story was the product of the running away from home; the stress must have pushed poor Phoebe past the breaking point.

Phoebe would undergo years of therapy to cope with it. Overall, though, Phoebe's life developed more normally than one might expect. Episodes of paranoia were frequent at first but gradually decreased, and when they didn't afflict her, Phoebe's family was happy to have a very changed sister and daughter. She was pleasant—a word that would never have been used to describe her before—though she had developed a strange sudden interest in watching mixed martial arts on TV.

Antonia, of course, went on to shoot her movie and many others. She continued her careers as an athlete, actress, and model. She always intended to keep tabs on the others and she did for a little while. In fact, when she had a layover at the Ada County airport the next summer she invited the others to meet up with her for lunch in Boise. Jim, Axl, and Chuck were all able to come and all had a satisfying time together, though they were surprised when nobody brought up their strange experiences once in the entire visit. They were just friends catching up on one another's lives, ignoring the bleakness of the past and focusing on a much happier present and future. In fact, Antonia so quickly engrossed herself again in her old life that the four-day episode became nothing more than the unpleasant echo of a voice that Antonia was sure was fantasy. In her infrequent contact with the others she simply asked for updates, occasionally commenting on happy occasions in the others' lives like the birth of Chuck's daughter. It was only in Phoebe's occasional references to her "shrink" that Antonia was reminded of the circumstances under which she'd met her five new friends.

Axl went back to his family in Washington. He admitted a lot of the secrets he'd been keeping from his parents—the things he'd been eating, the things he'd tricked Uncle Jim into letting him do. But the events of those few days would always be a secret. He didn't want to see a psychiatrist (though realistically he knew he might need one in the future) and he definitely didn't want to be kept from his summertime visits to Uncle Jim's ranch. The adventure had been traumatic, it was true, but it had been an adventure and he'd survived it. And privately Axl counted his experience as a point of pride. He knew things nobody else knew, he'd done things nobody else had done, experienced things nobody else had experienced. He'd dug up a buried spaceship. He'd shot a monster dead in the mountains. It made him feel unique, special—and being special was just as good as being famous. Axl decided it was okay to be proud of those things even if he kept them a secret. Besides, Axl shared Uncle Jim's profound impression that their dealings with the supernatural were over—at least for the time being.

Jim stayed in Mackenzie. He had a feeling things were going to get right back to normal and they did. He and Juan went back to their renovations, his hired hands worked on making the property better suited for recreation, and Jim kept eating breakfast at Hometown Inn as long as it was open. Rumors came and went, but none were ever as exciting as Antonia LeBlanc eating breakfast at Hometown Inn. Jim was brought up sometimes as a possible participant in the Rumor of the Year. Some people said they'd seen him sitting with her and talking to her. "Could've been me," he always said, "but then again, there are a lot of old men with cowboy hats in Mackenzie."

Wildfire season came to Mackenzie, a bad one. A freak of a fire, though—it had started somewhere way up in the mountains near Minersville where people seldom went. Jim never said anything, but he was sure the fire had been intentional. He knew that somewhere up there were the ashes of an otherworldly aircraft and four dead giants.

He'd think about those four days sometimes, alone with his thoughts. For as long as the evenings were still warm Jim would wind down as the sun was setting on his front porch with only Brodie and the radio to keep him company. He toyed with the triangular coin on his key chain. Sam Cook was singing *A Change is Gonna Come.*

"Yep," Jim thought, "It sure is."

As much as they tried to stay away, all of them would find themselves back in that little nothing town in the years to come. Even Antonia—whose path in life would lead her to great fame and prestige, into history books and tabloids—would be led back to the very place she swore she'd never go again.

At the end of this chapter of the Mackenzie Experiments there were far more questions than answers. The future of Mackenzie, Idaho would be full of bizarre revelations. Some were being set in motion. Others had been in motion for hundreds of years.

Why, then, does the history of the Mackenzie Experiments begin here? Because this was when the veil of secrecy, so carefully set in place, began to unweave.

ABOUT THE AUTHOR

Dillon Flake grew up in rural Horseshoe Bend, Idaho. From a young age, he has been an avid writer and artist. This is his first published book.

Dillon lives in Provo, Utah with his wife, Emily, and daughter, Ruby. He is studying at Brigham Young University.

Made in the USA
Coppell, TX
07 February 2023